A Woman's Awakening

With the cloth dripping wet, she hurried to him,
then quickly knelt and applied it to his feverish brow,
his cheeks, and then his chest.

Suddenly Nicole felt the Indian shiver, whether in
pleasure or shock at the cold water, she didn't know.

She looked quickly at his eyes and grew pale when
she found them open again.

He was watching her every move.

She flinched, dropped the cloth, and crawled quickly away, stopping a few feet from him. Only then did
she turn to look at him again.

When their gazes met and held, Nicole felt a strange
reaction, like a butterfly fluttering inside her belly.

The Indian continued to gaze into her eyes, as
though he was looking far into her soul. His look gave
her a sudden, strange feeling of sensuality at the juncture of her thighs. She had never experienced such
feelings before.

It was an awakening of sorts, and it felt strangely
delicious.

CASSIE EDWARDS

SAVAGE DAWN

LEISURE BOOKS　　NEW YORK CITY

A LEISURE BOOK®

September 2009

Published by

Dorchester Publishing Co., Inc.
200 Madison Avenue
New York, NY 10016

ISBN 10: 0-8439-5880-4
ISBN 13: 978-0-8439-5880-5
E-ISBN: 978-1-4285-0726-5

The name "Leisure Books" and the stylized "L" with design are
trademarks of Dorchester Publishing Co., Inc.

Printed in the United States of America.

10 9 8 7 6 5 4 3 2 1

I dedicate Savage Dawn
To Annetta Marie Trumble, *a very special person
and the mother to my dear friend Linda Lum.*

*Always,
Cassie Edwards*

Poem

I know to love you is forbidden.
And so when it is day, I keep my
Thoughts of you hidden.
But when night falls, by the light of Sister
Moon, I run to you.
To the warmth of your skin to kiss you, to
breathe you in,
To once again feel your embrace,
To hold you and touch your beautiful face.
I run my fingers through your raven hair
And look into your eyes so brown.
I feel the love you have for me,
Words are spoken between us without a sound.
Our hearts beat fiercely as one,
With passion and true love.
This bond cannot be broken,
For it is united by the Great Spirit above.
My warrior, you are like the brightest star
Shining in the night,
You are my love, my light.
One day we shall stand together for all the world to see,
For you are my warrior and always will be.

By Sara Key, poet and friend

SAVAGE DAWN

Chapter One

A soft wind fluttered the closed entrance flap of the tepee as Chief Eagle Wolf sat beside his lodge fire on a warm autumn day. He had just made a terrible decision, one that he must now carry out to ensure the safety of his Navaho people.

Already, his Owl Clan had lost too many of its members. Only a few winters ago, his mother and father had been killed in a skirmish with the U.S. Cavalry. They had died as the Navaho fled the bluecoats who were trying to force them onto a reservation.

Many of their friends had died that day, as well, killed by the soldiers who brought death and destruction to Chief Eagle Wolf's beloved people.

What had remained of their Owl Clan had followed Eagle Wolf to this mountain stronghold, where they had found a safe haven in a deep, hidden canyon. From that time on, Eagle Wolf had taken leadership of his people, as his father had led them before his untimely death.

Eagle Wolf's midnight-dark eyes filled with deep

sadness as he stared into the dancing flames of the fire, remembering all that had happened to his people because of the white eyes. So much of it was *hogay-gahn*, bad.

When Eagle Wolf and his people had finally reached safety on this mountain, and had established their homes there, many of the Owl Clan had died from a disease white men had carried to Navaho land, an illness known to everyone as . . . smallpox.

Eagle Wolf had buried his wife, as well as many of his friends. And today he had discovered the same ugly spots on his own body.

To keep from exposing his people further to the disease that he now carried, Eagle Wolf had decided to flee the village. He would go off by himself, someplace where he could either die from the disease, or recover and then return to his people to resume his role as their chief.

His people had approved of his decision to temporarily turn the duties of chief over to his brother Spirit Wolf, who had seen five winters fewer than his own twenty-five. His brother understood that if Eagle Wolf came out of this situation alive, he would once more take on the title of chief.

Realizing that he had taken enough time pondering what had been, what was, and what might be, Eagle Wolf stood up and faced the closed entrance flap. Just beyond it, his brother stood awaiting Eagle Wolf's moment of departure.

Dressed in only a breechclout and moccasins, Eagle Wolf spoke through the buckskin covering of the entrance flap.

"My brother, it is time now for me to leave," he said sadly. His sculpted, copper face showed only a few of the dreaded spots, yet there were enough to make him realize that soon his whole body might be covered with the pox.

His muscled shoulders tightened as he bent low and picked up a leather sheath, in which lay his sharp knife. He attached this at the right side of his waist.

Then he gazed at his quiver of arrows, remembering the hours he had spent making them. His eyes turned to his large bow, and he was filled with remembrances of sitting beside his lodge fire with his father while Eagle Wolf carved designs of forest animals into the wood.

Those were precious, revered memories that would stay with him even into his old age, if the Great Spirit granted him the blessing of long life.

But for now, it seemed doubtful that he would survive this terrible disease. He had prayed to the Great Spirit that he would live and still have the capacity to lead his people and keep them safe from white eyes and anyone else who might prove to be their enemy.

"My brother, I will slit my lodge covering down the back and leave that way so that I will not come near you. I do not wish to expose you to this illness that faces our people like a coiled snake, ready to strike first one and then another," Eagle Wolf said thickly. "I will set fire to my lodge and burn it along with everything within it. No one must come in contact with my possessions, which may carry the disease on them. All that I will take from my lodge is a parfleche bag of supplies, my trusted bow and arrows, my rifle, and my knife. I will go far enough away so that none of our people will be exposed to this disease."

"My brother, I will watch over our people in your absence," Spirit Wolf replied solemnly. "I will pray for you. So will all of our people. Surely our prayers will bring you back to us, well and ready to be a part of our lives once again. Then we will be *ka-bike-hozhoni-bi*—happy evermore."

"What is planned in the beginning, even before we have taken our first breaths of life, will be," Eagle Wolf said, removing his knife from its sheath and slowly running its sharp edge down the buckskin fabric of his lodge. "If it is in the Great Spirit's plan that I will return to our people, so shall I return. If not, and I should die, I will go to meet those who have departed before me. I trust you, my brother, to make sure our people thrive in my absence. Most of all, keep them safe from any white eyes who might venture up our mountain."

"I shall do all that is expected of me," Spirit Wolf called, for he knew now that Eagle Wolf was no longer in his tepee, but instead at the back. He could smell the smoke as his brother set fire to the buckskin covering. "My brother, be safe. Be well!"

"Spirit Wolf, my body is only a shell," Eagle Wolf replied as he stepped away from the burning lodge, his bow slung over his left shoulder, his knife secured again in its sheath. His rifle was in its gun boot at the side of his white stallion, which he had tied behind his lodge. "Should I die, my spirit will survive and live on."

All went quiet, except for the popping and crackling of the fire as everything inside the tepee was consumed by flames.

He was filled with a keen sadness that all his belongings except for what he carried in his parfleche bag were going up in flames. Most of all, he hated to lose those things that had belonged to his dear wife, Precious Stone.

Feeling the heat of the flames on his face, Eagle Wolf watched for a moment longer, then turned and ran to his horse.

No, he had not enjoyed seeing the tepee and its contents going up in flames, but he knew that if he survived, he would return and build another one just as strong and large. He would then begin to accumulate personal belongings and wealth all over again.

The stench of his burning lodge followed him as Eagle Wolf mounted his white stallion and rode away from the canyon where he had brought his people to safety.

His eyes were bloodshot and aching. The spots on his face itched, especially now that the smoke had irritated them.

He felt suddenly sick to his stomach and he knew by touching his fiery brow that he had a raging temperature.

But he could not stop to rest until he was far enough away from his people so that they would be safe from the disease he carried in his body.

He must make his way far down the mountain pass, as far from his people as he could get. And once he found a safe place to stop, he must center his thoughts on getting well. He knew that his people needed and depended on him. His brother was a strong warrior and loved by their Owl Clan, too, but it was Eagle Wolf who had been taught the skills of leadership by his chieftain father.

Eagle Wolf's father had begun teaching him as soon as Eagle Wolf could retain the lessons in his mind and heart.

He vividly remembered the many hours he had spent with his father, listening with pride and love to the words of the wise Navaho chief. Eagle Wolf was taught in the same way his father was counseled by his own chieftain father.

Missing his father so much, Eagle Wolf was even more determined to get well and resume his role as chief; his father would not want it to be any other way.

Eagle Wolf was a man who did not cry easily,

but at this moment he could feel the heat of tears in his eyes as he remembered his father.

He looked heavenward. He knew that his father was there now, in spirit, looking over him and giving Eagle Wolf the strength and courage that it would take for him to return to his people a well man.

"And so I shall," he whispered as he began his descent.

He passed through a lovely forest of juniper, spruce and cedar trees, where the air was filled with birdsong. He could hear small animals scampering away from his horse's approach. He observed the creatures of the forest, trying to focus on something besides the sense of loss that filled him with such a deep, hurtful sadness.

He smiled as he looked slowly around him, thinking as he had many times before that Mother Nature had blessed this mountain and all of the land below that lay in its shadow.

It was a place where he sometimes saw antelope peacefully grazing. His favorite animal was the white-tailed deer; the most feared were the bears and cougars.

The beauty of this land and its animals never ceased to take his breath away, for each creature had its place in the order of things. Even the slinking wolf could be seen as beautiful by a man filled with the love of nature.

He had found a wounded wolf one day not long ago while he was riding along the mountain pass.

It was apparent that it had fought a fierce battle with an enemy. It had a large, raw wound on its right side, yet the wolf had apparently managed to escape the final death blow from its attacker.

Loving all animals, especially one that had proven to be so valiant as this wolf, Eagle Wolf had stopped his horse and dismounted. He had searched out and found a forest plant that his father had taught him was used for healing.

Eagle Wolf had torn the plant into tiny pieces and sprinkled the herb onto the wolf's open wound.

At first the wolf had snarled and bared its teeth at Eagle Wolf, but after he had spoken softly to it, the animal had stretched out and allowed Eagle Wolf to minister to its wounds.

Since then, Eagle Wolf believed that he had seen that same wolf from time to time, disappearing into the dark shadows of the forest as Eagle Wolf approached on his horse.

On those occasions, Eagle Wolf had felt the animal's yellow eyes on him, watching from its hiding place. Eagle Wolf could only smile, for he believed that the animal recognized him and saw him as a friend.

As he rode along now, Eagle Wolf searched the darkest shadows, wondering if that same wolf could be nearby?

Eagle Wolf had reached the lower part of the pass, and he was feeling dizzy from the fever. He knew that he could not go much farther. He needed to stop and rest.

He needed to find water so that he could bathe his face. He needed to recover so he could return to his people. There were many dangers still facing them.

His thoughts returned to the white government. The cavalry in charge at Fort Sumner had forced many Navaho people onto the reservation. But under Chief Eagle Wolf's leadership, the Owl Clan had escaped to this remote, high mountain.

His father had told him some winters ago that the mountain had special powers, powers that would serve their people well. His father had told Eagle Wolf that the mountain would work as a protective shield if ever they needed to seek sanctuary there. Hidden within its canyons, the clan would never be found by the white eyes. The spirits of the mountain would not allow it.

After his father's death, Eagle Wolf had led their people up this mountain, where they had established new homes in the deep slash of a canyon.

He and his people met often in their council house. There they offered prayers to the mountain, asking the spirits to keep them all safe.

Thus far, the mountain had continued to bless them. Except for this disease that the white man had passed to his people, the Owl Clan had remained safe.

Their hunts were always bountiful and their gardens provided vegetables for their cook pots.

Ho, except for the disease that Eagle Wolf was carrying away from his people, life had been good for the Owl Clan in the place they named Navaho Mountain.

"It will be our home, always, whether or not I am there to experience its goodness myself," Eagle Wolf whispered to himself.

But for now he must find a place to stay where he could battle this disease alone and away from those he loved.

He gazed into the blue sky and prayed again for his body to heal.

Chapter Two

The stagecoach rumbled onward, sending dust through the window to the interior, where Nicole Tyler sat with seven other passengers, squeezed in like sardines in a can. She tried to focus on anything but how uncomfortable and hot she was, yet it was hard. It was autumn, when the days could turn from cold to hot in the blink of an eye.

Today was one of the most uncomfortable, hottest autumn days that Nicole could recall. It was torment sharing the tiny space of the coach with so many people.

As they sat squeezed together, inhaling each other's body aromas, Nicole squirmed uncomfortably on the hard seat.

She was a beautiful girl, her hair the color of the fiery red setting sun she had witnessed so often from her home in Missouri. Her eyes were the color of the lush green grass in spring. Her face was oval, her cheeks were a lovely pink, and her lashes were thick and long. She drew attention wherever she went.

Today she wore a dark cotton floor-length travel skirt and a white long-sleeved blouse that did nothing for the shapely curves beneath her attire.

For the most part, she could be defined as petite, but she had been blessed with those attributes that drew too many a man's notice, as far as she was concerned.

All that she wanted out of life was to be left alone to find her own happiness. Ever since she had been old enough to understand how a teacher shaped children's lives sometimes even more than their parents, it had been her dream to teach. She wanted to help make children's lives fulfilling and happy.

Soon this dream would come true, and she was delighted at the prospect.

She longed to be a teacher even more than she wanted to be a wife. Up until now, no man had interested her.

Ignoring the only man in the stagecoach today, and the way he seemed to fix his eyes on her much too often, she held on to the seat as she stared through the window.

As they passed beneath the welcome shade of tall and stately trees on both sides of the road, all she could think about was how anxious she was to get to Tyler City, where she would be reunited with her mother and father.

She loved her parents, but often during her

childhood, she had been given cause to question her father's choices in life.

Most of her friends adored their fathers, but *her* father was vastly different from her friends'.

He had cheated his way into wealth by his skill at gambling. In fact, he had amassed enough money to leave their home in St. Louis, Missouri, and had bought up land in Utah, enough land to build a whole town.

Nicole's face flushed red even now as she recalled the reason why they had left St. Louis. Her father had cheated at cards one time too many, and the leaders of that fine city had told him that if he didn't take himself elsewhere, they would lock him up and throw away the key!

Her father had heard about Utah, with its green valleys, towering mountains, and rivers teeming with fish. His favorite pastime after playing poker was fishing.

Nicole had accompanied her father many a time when he went fishing in the muddy waters of the mighty Mississippi River. She had brought in many a delicious catfish that her mother had cooked and placed on the evening dining table.

She wondered whether her father was enjoying the fishing in Utah. Had he truly been able to put his gambling days behind him and enjoy spending time with his wife, whom he had often neglected while gambling was the most prominent thing on his mind?

Her mother had not enjoyed fishing or boating, so she had not shared those rare moments when Nicole joined her father on the river, laughing and talking.

Nicole had seen her mother smile with joy when Nicole's father had told her that he was through with gambling and that he would build her a whole town in Utah that she could all her own!

It would be named after their family.

It would be called . . . Tyler City.

It had been decided that Nicole would stay in St. Louis until she finished her schooling and received her teaching credentials. Until only a few weeks ago, she had lived with her aunt Dot and uncle Zeb.

But now?

Having finally earned her teaching credentials, she was anxious to join her mother and father in Tyler City.

Her father had told her that with the town so new, everything from doctors to teachers were needed.

She would be the first teacher!

She had begun her journey west on a riverboat. Oh, how slow it had been.

After smelling the stench of fish that wafted in from the river, she had been glad to board a stagecoach for the final leg of the trip. Even now the smell of fish seemed to cling to her skin and clothes.

But it had been rugged traveling since she had

boarded the stagecoach. She ached all over, especially her behind.

The voices of children broke through her thoughts, bringing her eyes to the four little girls who had been silent for most of the trip.

But now their father had announced that they had almost reached their destination, a new, small town called Hope. Their excitement at this news showed in their lovely eyes and high voices.

Suddenly their father ordered them to silence, scolding that they were bothering the young lady.

Nicole almost spoke up to tell him that it mattered not to her if the girls were talking, but decided against it. After spending so many hours in the coach with this man, she knew that his word was law to his family. To them he was almost a god!

Her fellow travelers were a family of Mormons, which included four little girls and two wives. The man's name was Jeremiah Schrock, and his wives' names were Nancy and Martha.

But Nicole had not been told the names of the girls. When she had entered the stagecoach, the man had introduced himself to her, as well as his two wives. From that point on he had remained silent except for when he found reason to scold one daughter or the other.

Though he did not speak to her, he continued to give Nicole looks that made her very uncomfortable. He was a man of fine appearance, with a

square jaw that was prominent even though he
wore a beard.

He had sparkling blue eyes, and was dressed in
a suit of black that revealed muscles bulging
against the tightness of the fabric. Nicole knew
that he was the sort to attract many a woman's
eyes to him.

But not her. She hated the way he looked her
up and down, as though he might be sizing her
up to be his third wife!

That thought repelled her. This man had already taken two wives, seemed to enjoy lording it
over them. She had no desire to be the third.

During this long trip on the stagecoach, Nicole had avoided the man's stares by gazing out
the window, while feeling pity for the poor things
that he had already claimed as his.

They were timid women, who hardly spoke
a word during their entire time in the stagecoach.

She now looked out the window just in time to
see that the stagecoach was approaching the small
town of Hope, where a small community of Mormons had been established.

Nicole strained her neck to see as much as she
could of the place. She found it to be a lovely,
quiet community of small, yet pretty, houses, all
painted white.

Many children were running around outside,
laughing and playing. She saw women hanging

wash on lines. She saw a vast garden planted with everything needed for survival.

Just as the stagecoach drew to a stop, Nicole smiled and waved from the window to a little girl. The child stared back at her from between a man and woman whom Nicole concluded were her parents.

Nicole flinched when one of the wives who was departing the stagecoach, the one named Nancy, stepped on Nicole's foot. She realized quickly that it was no accident when Nancy glared at her as she stopped to meet Nicole's gaze.

This woman had quietly sat by as her husband measured Nicole's appeal, but she was obviously seething at the idea that Nicole might be her husband's third wife.

Nicole wanted to tell Nancy that she would never consider joining their family, but kept silent as the woman joined the others outside. The members of the small community took turns embracing the new comers.

The girls were soon gone, holding hands with new friends, giggling, as they ran off to play.

The stagecoach lurched forward, jarring Nicole so much that she almost fell from the seat. She settled in again for the rest of the journey, thank goodness, this time alone.

She smiled as she thought about what lay ahead . . . her family's very own town. She envisioned it being neat and pretty, and as peaceful as the Mormon town that was now far behind her and soon forgotten.

Sighing in relief at having the coach all to herself, Nicole was pleased to see that she was now traveling through a beautiful setting of lush trees and thick, green grass.

She enjoyed smelling the scent of flowers that grew wild amidst the grass. Their varied colors gave the countryside the look of a patchwork quilt.

She gazed farther from the window and saw one of the tallest mountains she had ever beheld.

She had been told about this mountain before boarding the stagecoach. It was said that many Navaho people lived on it, renegades who had gone there to avoid conflict with the U.S. government.

She had heard that the Navaho had fled high up on that mountain to be safe from the cavalry, and also other enemy tribes.

She shivered as she recalled someone saying, too, that no one but the Navaho should go on that mountain or they might wind up being scalped.

Suddenly her thoughts were interrupted by the shocking sight of rolling black smoke in the distance.

What alarmed her most was that the smoke was coming from the direction of Tyler City.

She stiffened when she heard the approach of a horse. A lone rider came up to the side of the stagecoach and shouted at the driver that he should turn the stagecoach around and drive quickly back in the direction they had came from. He told them to flee for their lives, and Nicole felt sick inside when he explained why.

He was saying that things had gone crazy in Tyler City.

Murder!

Mayhem!

The stagecoach driver wasted no time making a wide, shaky turn with the stagecoach.

When Nicole realized that she wasn't going to be taken to Tyler City after all, she stuck her head out the window and shouted at the driver.

"Stop!" she cried. "Please turn back. You must go on to Tyler City! You can't leave those who are alive there stranded. You must go and help them. My . . . parents . . . are there. Please?"

"Not on your life, lady," the driver shouted back at her. The stagecoach was now headed away from the burning inferno behind them. "Get your head back inside! Shut your mouth! I'm not ready to lose my scalp. Don't you know it's Injuns that are responsible for what's happened there."

Realizing that nothing she said would convince the driver to go to Tyler City, she knew that all that she could do now was try to convince him to stop and lend her a horse so that she could ride there, herself.

While she had lived with her aunt Dot and uncle Zeb in St. Louis, her uncle had taught her how to ride, and she was now as good as any cowpoke who might challenge her to a race.

"If you won't take me to Tyler City, please at least lend me a horse so that I can go there myself," Nicole shouted.

Her hair blew around her face and whipped against her cheeks.

She brushed it aside as she waited for either the driver or the guard to answer her.

The man who had warned of the devastation up ahead had already raced off to safety.

"Please, oh, please, at least do that for me," Nicole cried when the men still didn't respond to her. "My mother and father are in Tyler City. In fact, it's my father's town, established by him, and named after our family."

That drew the driver's attention.

He gave her a strange, pitying look, then drew the horses to a shuddering halt.

Nicole saw this as a positive sign. She grabbed her reticule and hurried out the coach just as the driver jumped down to stand beside her.

"It's your scalp, lady," he said, nervously shuffling his feet. "Guess I can spare one horse if'n you can cough up enough money to pay for it."

Her heart pounding, Nicole opened the reticule and grabbed a handful of coins. "That's all I have with me," she said, searching the man's dark eyes as she held the coins toward him in the palm of her hand. "Please say it's enough. I truly must go and see how my parents are."

He stared for a moment longer into her eyes,

looked at the coins, then shrugged and took the money.

As he shoved the coins into his front right breeches pocket, he hurried to the team of horses.

"I think you're mighty foolish," he said, as he finally separated a brown mare from the others. "It's no skin off'n my back whatever you do, for the horses don't belong to me, but the stagecoach company. I'll just tell 'em this mare was stole by a bunch of Injun renegades."

He placed a bridle and reins on the horse and led it to Nicole. "I think you should think again about what you're going to do," he said, before handing the reins over to her. "It sounds like bad trouble in that town."

"I know," Nicole murmured. She swallowed hard and glanced at her bag of belongings lashed to the top of the stagecoach. In it were her teaching certificate as well as other things precious to her.

She started to mount the horse, bareback, but stopped when the man who rode with the stage-coach as its guard pitched Nicole a rifle and a small leather bag of ammunition.

"I wouldn't sleep nights if'n I hadn't given you something to protect yourself with," he said thickly. "I just wish you'd reconsider."

The driver came with a saddle that he carried with him on his trips, secured it to the horse, and then got Nicole's travel bag and attached it at the side of the saddle.

"You are too kind," Nicole said as she opened her bag and wedged the rifle into it, with only the butt sticking up in the air.

She hurriedly mounted the mare, gave the men a quivering smile, then rode off in the direction of the black, rolling smoke.

She was afraid that she might already be too late to help her parents.

Her jaw tightened when she thought of something else.

Was her father somehow responsible for what had happened in Tyler City? Had he gone back on his word and begun gambling again? Had he cheated one man too many?

Although her father had promised Nicole's mother that his gambling days were over and done with, deep down inside, Nicole had always believed that was impossible.

When gambling got as deep in a man's gut as it had her father's, there was no way on earth that he'd ever be able to look the other way if he was challenged to a game of poker.

Chapter Three

Feeling sick to his stomach from the raging temperature that had invaded his body, Eagle Wolf drew rein beside a stream.

He dismounted from his horse and stumbled to the water, falling to his knees beside it.

He hung his head over the water, but nothing came from his stomach. He had actually wanted to vomit so that he might feel a little better.

He raised his head and gasped when he saw his reflection in the water. His face was flushed from the fever and he knew that he must find a place to rest while he battled the disease that had weakened his body.

With knees trembling and broad shoulders drooping, he turned and looked at the place his horse had brought him. He had ridden the last mile with his eyes half closed, his ability to reason all but gone.

He had just hung on to the reins and let his horse take him where it would.

It seemed to Eagle Wolf that his steed had

sensed the importance of finding the right sanctuary for the man who had always treated him so well.

His stallion seemed to have understood the need for Eagle Wolf to be in a place where he could rest and get well without having to concern himself with passersby. The animal had brought him to a small, hidden canyon, where there was plenty of water from a stream trickling out of cracks in the mountainside, and where there were soft pine needles upon which he could sleep.

Not taking time to build a campfire, he secured his horse's reins, then took a blanket from his travel bag.

Just as he had spread the blanket on the soft pine needles, and had turned to lie down, something in the distance caught his eye.

He crept over to the edge of the bluff that overlooked the land below.

In the distance he could see black, rolling smoke and he quickly realized where it was coming from.

He knew of a small town that had recently been established not far from Navaho Mountain. It was a town called Tyler City.

Word had been brought to him that the man who established this town was a well-known gambler who had come to this area from a place named St. Louis.

Eagle Wolf knew that the reputation of such gamblers followed them wherever they went, and trouble followed them, too. There was always someone ready to challenge the one who was said to be the best.

Eagle Wolf had heard that often such duels with cards led to duels with firearms . . . and death. He wondered if this time someone had gotten angry enough to set fire to the entire town.

He watched the flames rolling upward from first one building and then another, as the smoke billowed into the sky.

If he were not alone, and he were well, he would ride down to that place of devastation and see if there were any survivors who needed help. Although he hated the U.S. government and its pony soldiers, he did not bear ill will toward the ordinary people, who had nothing to do with the decisions that had almost destroyed his tribe.

But as it was, he was alone, and his warriors were many miles up the mountain. And even if his warriors were close enough for him to go to them, he was not strong enough, either in body or mind, to even ride in his saddle now.

Suddenly he saw a lone rider traveling hard on a magnificent steed, toward the burning town.

He wiped at eyes that were blurring with fever, hoping to get a better look. When he lowered his hand, he realized that the lone rider was not a man, but instead . . . a woman!

He was awestruck by the woman's long red hair, which fluttered and blew in the wind behind her as she raced onward, obviously intent on arriving in the burning town as quickly as she could.

He wondered what she was doing alone when danger lay everywhere. A lone woman attracted the worst kind of men, those who would not hesitate to take advantage of her.

Where had this woman come from? He saw no other riders anywhere.

Suddenly he was overcome by dizziness. The land below him became a swirling mass.

He knew that he was in danger of falling if he did not lie down. He must concentrate on his own welfare now. Whatever happened below could not concern him.

He must think of himself now, for he had his people's future to think about. He must get well so that he could return to them.

Even though he loved his brother, something in Eagle Wolf's heart told him Spirit Wolf could not altogether be trusted. Lately his brother had looked at him with a strangeness in his dark eyes.

But this was not the time to concern himself with his suspicious. When Eagle Wolf returned home, he would look into his brother's strange behavior.

He stumbled back to where he had spread the blanket over a soft bed of pine needles.

He eased down onto the blanket, and almost the moment he closed his eyes, he was fast asleep. But his sleep was not peaceful.

He dreamed.

He groaned.

He tossed and turned.

Suddenly he awakened in a sweat.

He did not feel as feverish as he had before going to sleep. But the weakness that had claimed him now was a new enemy.

Again he closed his eyes, and this time he slept more peacefully.

When he began dreaming anew, he saw the woman on the horse again, but this time her red hair was swirling all around her and her steed, fully enveloping them both. The woman's hair was so beautiful as the sun shone on it, making it an even deeper red.

In his dream he saw the color of the woman's eyes, which were as green as fresh spring grass.

And her lips. They were red, too, and oh, so perfectly shaped, as though they were made to be kissed.

He could not see much more than that since her long, flowing hair hid the rest of her. But his senses were so keen in this dream, he could actually smell the woman's sweetness, as though she had bathed in the petals of the roses that grew wild along the plains.

His breathing was more even now. His body seemed to ache less. He settled into a deeper sleep.

In these moments of restful slumber, he would

find his strength again so he could return to his people a well man.

Yet . . . something made him want to find the woman first.

Chapter Four

Fighting the sting in her eyes caused by the pervasive black smoke, Nicole came to a stop as she entered what had for a short time been a town named after her family.

A sob caught in her throat when she looked around her. All of the buildings, which had been few, were either already burned to the ground or burning rapidly.

Nothing had been spared, and no one.

She gulped hard as she tried not to vomit. There were dead bodies everywhere. She saw men, women, and children who had been viciously murdered.

"No!" she cried to the heavens as everything in her rebelled when she caught sight of the two people she had loved so dearly lying nearby.

"Mama, Papa . . ." she gasped.

Her heart seemed to stop the instant she saw them, lying side by side, on their backs.

She choked up with deep emotion when she saw that they were holding hands. It was such a touching scene, for in death they seemed to have found the truth of their love for each other.

But when she saw how they had been killed, Nicole's heart pounded and her face grew hot with a mixture of emotions—sadness, regret, pain, but most of all, hate for whoever had done this to her parents.

Each had been shot with a single bullet in the forehead, execution style. Nicole almost fainted from the shock of it.

Her despair was so overwhelming, she suddenly wished now that she had been with her parents, and had died with them. Living without them, alone, would be worse than death. How could she go on, knowing her parents had died in such a way?

But she again focused on their clasped hands. That lone gesture of love made their deaths more bearable for Nicole. When she was overwhelmed with sadness and loneliness without them, she would remember the love her parents had shared as they took their last breaths of life.

Sobbing, she slid from her saddle and started to go and kneel beside her parents to say a prayer. She stopped, her heart almost coming to a standstill in her chest, when she saw movement out of the corner of her eyes.

Nicole turned quickly.

She was breathless with hope when she saw a man stirring on the ground not far from where her parents lay. He was alive!

Out of all this murder and mayhem . . . a man had survived.

At that realization, Nicole felt a surge of resentment toward this man for having lived while her parents had not. But being a Christian, she felt sudden shame at her uncharitable feeling and hurried to the man to see if there was anything she could do for him.

She knelt at his side. But as she did, she realized just how badly the man had been wounded.

Through the blood on his shirt, she saw that he had been shot in the belly. She knew that was one of the worst places to be shot, and that most times the victim did not survive.

Suddenly he reached out for Nicole's hand and grabbed it. She could feel his trembling, yet there was a strange sort of determination in his grip. She saw that same determination in his eyes as he looked anxiously up at her through tears that were now streaming from his eyes.

"I'm so sorry," Nicole struggled to say between her own sobs. "I am so truly sorry. I wish I could do something. Your name. What's your name?"

She felt inadequate, knowing this was the only thing she could think to say to this man who was surely in so much pain, and whose breath could stop at any moment.

Surely he had more important things to say than his name! But what could be important if you knew you were dying?

Would he be thinking of his family? Was he

wondering how they were? Would he ask her to search for them?

Her thoughts were interrupted when the man finally managed to speak.

"Harold Jones. My . . . name . . . is Harold . . . Jones," he gasped, as he struggled to talk through the pain that was obviously gripping him. "Listen. Before I die, you must listen to what I have to say. You . . . need . . . to know that . . . it was white men who did this . . . not Injuns."

Nicole noticed that he winced with each word spoken, as though a knife was stabbing into his wound. She felt the same pain, even though she had no wound except the one in her heart created by her losses!

Harold stopped and drew in a quivering breath, closed his eyes for a moment, but still held Nicole's hand tightly.

Then he looked up at her again.

"Those men . . . they . . . looked innocent enough when they rode into town," he continued, yet with a voice that grew fainter by the minute. "I must get this told. You need to know. Tell those who can do something about it."

"I will," Nicole gulped out as she looked quickly over her shoulder at her parents, and then back into Harold's eyes. "I promise I will."

"I was in the saloon when they came in," Harold continued. "I was at the bar, drinking. The men, five of them, went over to the poker table and sat down. They started up a card game with

Mr. Tyler. I . . . I . . . knew there would be trouble from the beginning. I could tell that one of those men had a grudge against Mr. Tyler."

Nicole gasped again and felt the color drain from her face at hearing her father's name. Harold stopped and studied her expression, but seeming to sense he had little time left on this earth, he continued.

"Suddenly everything went crazy. One of the men accused Mr. Tyler of cheating, saying Mr. Tyler had cheated before, too," Harold said, his voice now barely a whisper.

Nicole listened with an aching heart, for she now knew without a doubt that her father had not kept his word about never gambling again.

"The man who accused Mr. Tyler of cheating said he'd not get the chance to cheat him again, or anyone else," Harold said. "Mr. Tyler knew the man meant business and managed to flee the saloon before the other gambler got his first shot at him. I . . . I . . . followed the gambler and his men out of the building 'cause I knew that all hell was ready to break loose. Suddenly Mr. Tyler's wife was there. They . . . were both shot."

Harold gasped in pain and paused. Nicole could tell that he was struggling now with every breath and expected him to die at any moment.

His hand weakened in hers. "I must . . . get . . . it said," he said, his eyes now closed. "The strangers killed everyone in town. It was a massacre.

They spared no one. The leader of this murderous gang? I caught one of the men calling him by name just before that same man turned and fired a bullet into my gut. The leader's name . . . was . . . Sam Partain."

After speaking the name of the man who had ordered the killings, Harold Jones gasped again, drew in a shuddering breath, and then died.

As his hand dropped away from hers, Nicole watched his body grow limp, his eyes now looking back at her with a death stare.

Her hands trembling, she reached out and slowly closed his eyes. "I'm so sorry," she whispered. "May the good Lord be with you."

Sobbing, she slowly stood up and went back to where her parents lay.

Fortunately their eyes were closed so that she wouldn't have to look into them and see death.

Weak now from shock and despair, she knelt beside them. Smoke still billowed into the sky and ash now blew in the wind, swirling like small tornadoes along the death-ridden ground.

Nicole gazed at her father. "How could you have lied?" she whispered, remembering the very moment he had promised he would never gamble again, and how sincerely he had said it to Nicole and her mother.

"Papa, if you only knew the worst of it," she said sadly. "You are responsible for the deaths of these people who trusted you enough to move into your town. It is all because of you and your love of gambling. Even my precious mother, your beloved wife, paid for your . . . your . . . stupidity, your sins!"

She closed her eyes to try to compose herself, and while they were closed, the name that Harold had spoken to her flashed into her mind.

"Sam Partain," she said aloud, her eyes opening quickly as she looked into the distance, where the murderers had no doubt disappeared.

She looked down at her father again. "Papa, I remember that name," she murmured. "He is that gambler you bragged about having beaten in poker more than once. Papa, apparently Sam Partain tracked you down and gambled this one last time with you. But this time, Papa, you were the loser. You lost your life."

Again Nicole looked around her, truly afraid when a sudden thought came to her like a slap in the face.

Sam Partain held a grudge against her, too. She had met him once or twice and had been repelled by his rough ways. When he'd tired to cozy up to her, she'd turned a cold shoulder.

She remembered now his angry reaction to her rejection.

She gazed down at her father again. "Oh, Papa, I pray that while you were gambling with Sam Partain you didn't say anything about me being on my way to town," she said, her voice drawn. "I . . . I . . . know how you loved bragging about your only daughter."

Sam Partain had killed everyone who had anything to do with her father. Nicole truly feared that he might feel the need to take her life, too.

If so, he might even at this moment be looking for her. He might be nearby.

She was afraid that he might not rest until he saw that Nicole joined her parents in death.

Yes, she must leave. And soon. But first she must say a little prayer over her parents' bodies.

She knew that she couldn't chance taking the time to bury them. She was too afraid that Sam might even now be watching her from a distance.

Sobbing, Nicole buried her face in her hands. Through her sobs she whispered a soft prayer. Then, as her eyes slowly opened, she saw something in her father's vest pocket that made her aching sadness turn to sudden anger. There, in full view, was a pack of playing cards.

Her father had promised never to gamble again!

He had lied!

Her fingers trembling, Nicole yanked the cards from his pocket and threw them into the wind.

She gazed at her father's clean-shaven face, which was now covered with his own life's blood. The hole in his forehead was a hideous reminder of the violent way he and her mother had died.

She could not help wondering which of them had been the first to be shot, while the other helplessly watched!

Not wanting to think any more about the details of this horrible massacre, she stood up quickly.

She looked through the smoke at the mountain that was visible not far from what remained of Tyler City.

She would find protection there, and when she felt it was safe enough, she would ride to the closest fort, or town, where she could report the massacre.

But for now, she must hide. She ran to her horse and mounted it.

All she knew about this mountain was that it was inhabited by Navaho Indians. She was aware that she should be afraid of Indians, but at this moment, she was more afraid of Sam Partain.

She had read in a St. Louis newspaper about all sorts of atrocities that Indians were guilty of. But so far, on her way to Tyler City, she had seen no Indians. She had spotted some smoke signals high in the mountains, but that was all.

Was she being foolish to ride right into Navaho territory? A cold shiver rode her spine at the thought of coming face-to-face with an Indian.

Yet still she turned her steed in the direction of the mountain and without a last look at what she must leave behind her on the cold ground, she rode away, to a new life. She was deeply afraid that her future would be lonely and filled with danger.

Chapter Five

As soon as Eagle Wolf had departed the village, his brother had set about constructing a new tepee for him. Spirit Wolf wanted to surprise Eagle Wolf with a new home when he returned, instead of waiting for Eagle Wolf to rebuild. Now Spirit Wolf was basking in the newness of the huge buckskin tepee.

He would enjoy being his people's chief while he could, for he had no doubt that Eagle Wolf would get well and soon return to reclaim the title.

Spirit Wolf was dressed in clothes made from deerskin, a fringed shirt, leggings, and heavily beaded moccasins, his shiny black hair drawn back into a long braid down his back. He sat on the floor of the new tepee on a rich, thick mat of bear fur.

The glow from the lodge fire in the center of the tepee was a little too warm on this autumn day, but he was enjoying this moment alone, savoring the feel of power.

As he gazed at the flames rolling slowly over

the logs in the firepit, he could not help imagining all sorts of benefits that would come with being temporary chief.

He could even envision something that his brother talked against . . . warring with whites.

Spirit Wolf felt different from his brother. Spirit Wolf hungered for war. He would proudly lead the warriors of his clan into battle!

He had always felt the strong need to fight, not only with white enemies, but also any of the other tribes who threatened his Owl Clan.

Ho, he would defeat the enemies of his people in battle and then rightfully claim the title of chief. He would prove his worth, prove he was more worthy of being chief than his brother. Eagle Wolf had backed away from war and brought their people to this mountain to hide.

Hiding went against Spirit Wolf's nature, yet because he was not the true chief, he had to accept whatever his brother decided was best to keep their people safe.

"And they are safe," Spirit Wolf whispered to himself as he stretched his legs out and crossed them at the ankles. "But will they always be so? Or will the white eyes finally decide to come onto the mountain and challenge our Owl Clan?"

If so, Spirit Wolf would step forth and lead the battle against them!

Ho, Spirit Wolf could not deny how he enjoyed his daydreams of being chief.

He closed his eyes and smiled as he listened to

the children at play outside in the shadow of the tall bluff that stood at the backside of the stronghold.

Pretending that he was the true chief, Spirit Wolf listened to the voices of some elderly men as they traded stories beside an outdoor fire while smoking their long-stemmed pipes.

He heard some women chattering like magpies, sitting together outside one of their lodges, speaking of things they had done today, or possibly even discussing their chief and the illness that had sent him away from their village.

Knowing he now led all these people, Spirit Wolf felt important, more so than he ever had in his life.

Ho, he had always been second to his brother, since he was the younger of the two. It had always been known which brother would be their Owl Clan's leader once their father passed on to the other world.

Because of that knowledge, everyone spoke more of Eagle Wolf. People had looked up to him early on, even before it was time for him to become their chief.

Spirit Wolf was not certain when resentment against his brother began to grow inside his heart. But it was there.

Recently those feelings had become more intense. Envy ate away at his insides when he saw that his brother was treated with more respect and awe than himself, even though Spirit Wolf had always tried to prove his own worth to his people.

"It is *hogay-gahn*. It is wrong that nothing I have ever done, or said, changed anything," he whispered bitterly to himself. "Nothing."

But now things had changed. However, the change would benefit Spirit Wolf only if his brother did not return to reclaim his title.

Upon Eagle Wolf's return, everything would go back to the way if had been. *Ho*, Spirit Wolf would again be made to walk in his brother's shadow. And he would continue there either until his brother's death, or Spirit Wolf's own.

Death did seem to be the only answer, but it was not something he wanted to think about. If his brother succumbed to this disease that had forced him to leave his people, then Spirit Wolf would finally achieve what he never could otherwise!

"Chief Spirit Wolf," he whispered to himself, testing the sound of the title as it passed his lips.

Again he smiled. "*Ho*, I like it," he whispered. "And so shall everyone else when they have no other choice but to accept me as their chief."

He fought off the guilt that came with actually wishing his brother would die.

Spirit Wolf had never shown any outward signs of resenting his brother; he knew those who witnessed such behavior would turn their backs on him in disgust.

So he had carried this secret well guarded inside his heart; even his brother had never seen any hint of resentment when he looked at Spirit Wolf.

Ho, now was the time for Spirit Wolf to be the object of everyone's attention. Even those who were the most devoted to their true chief, Eagle Wolf, would see the worth of his younger brother.

Spirit Wolf had cleverly aligned himself with warriors who he knew could be encouraged to follow his leadership, no matter what. If Eagle Wolf did live and return take up his old position, it would be brother against brother.

Spirit Wolf planned to be the victor!

He looked one last time around him, at the big new tepee. If his brother did return, this new lodge would be his, at least until Spirit Wolf got brave enough to do what he must to take leadership from his brother.

But for now, Spirit Wolf had another place to be. His own new lodge, which had also recently been erected. He would return to it and to his new bride.

When his people had fled to this mountain hideaway they had been joined by members of a different clan who were rescued along with Spirit Wolf's own people and brought to live among them.

Spirit Wolf had chosen a young and beautiful maiden from among those people. He had married her. He saw in her the perfect wife who would bear him many sons. To him, sons were far more important than daughters; it was necessary to have enough men to defend the future of their clan.

Oh, but he did love his new bride. She was the only person in his life who had ever won his loyalty. Spirit Wolf had grown to love her, with a love so overwhelming, he knew that this woman was the most positive force in his life right now.

This beautiful, delicate creative, whom he loved with every fiber of his being, was his now, no matter what else happened in his life. And she had a name that matched her loveliness.

Her name was Dancing Snow Feather!

Chapter Six

The campfire burned softly as the meat of a deer cooked on a spit over it, thick and juicy.

Sam Partain and his gang were washing in the river not far from the clearing where the food cooked and their horses were tethered.

They were laughing and splashing each other as they bathed the smell of death and smoke from their bodies.

"We got the son of a gun," bragged Ace, one of Sam's men, his long stringy black hair resting on his shiny, wet, muscled shoulders. "Did you see the look in that gambler's eyes when you first shot his wife in the head, then aimed the gun at him? You've been itchin' to kill that son of a gun for a long time, and you did, Sam. Good for you. Good for you."

"He didn't die all that quickly," Sam grumbled as he ran his fingers through his thick blond hair. He was a tall, thin man, with shaggy whiskers. "If I had it to do over, I'd have shot him again in order to keep him from taking hold of his wife's hand like he did. I wanted him to spend eternity alone, damn him."

"The main thing to be glad of is that no one is left alive to tell what we did, and that we are far enough away from that stinking town not to be blamed for the killings," Ace said. "As it is, there ain't no chance in hell of anyone bein' on our trail, because we made certain that everyone was dead."

"But there is one thing left undone," Sam said as he climbed from the river and squeezed water from his hair.

"And what's that?" asked Tom, another one of the gang members, as he climbed out and stood beside Sam.

"The daughter of that cheatin' polecat gambler," Sam said, stepping into his breeches, and then pulling a shirt over his head.

"Why mess with her?" Tom asked as he quickly dressed, too. "We're lucky we got away with what we done with no one bein' the wiser. Why take the risk of searchin' for the woman?"

"Because I am a gambler, that's why," Sam growled as he sauntered over to the campfire and pressed a finger into the hot meat, checking it for tenderness.

"We're better off the way we left things," Ace said, sitting down on a blanket and pulling his boots on as the other men came from the river, water running from their flesh.

"I ain't gonna rest until I complete my mission," Sam said, sitting and pulling his own boots on.

"Mission?" Ace asked, squinting his eyes.

"Yep, mission," Sam said, combing his fingers through his hair to remove the tangles. "Before that gambler died, I forced the truth outta him about where his daughter, Nicole, was. She openly snubbed me back in St. Louie one time too many. The bitch. I swore to myself that I would get even with her for that. Well, I now know that she is on her way to Tyler City. She could arrive any day. I plan to be nearby when she arrives. Soon as I get my belly filled with deer, I'm leavin', and so are all of you, to find that smart-breeches of a daughter."

"We got away without bein' caught and now you plan to go back to Tyler City because of a mere woman?" Tom asked, raising his eyebrows.

"Not a mere woman," Sam grumbled. "Walter Tyler's daughter. She's the last piece of the revenge I planned to make Walter pay for makin' a fool out of me with his cheatin'."

"She ain't worth us all gettin' caught and taken to jail and hanged for the crimes we done," Ace said tightly. "Sam, you'd best rethink your plan. We're well off now. Let's just hightail it outta this area and find someone else to challenge with a game of poker."

Sam jumped to his feet.

He grabbed Ace by the throat and yanked him to his own feet.

Sam spoke tightly into Ace's face. "Now, you look here," he growled. "I'm the one who makes the plans. You are the one who helps me carry 'em out. If you want to challenge my right to lead this gang, well, all you have to do is say so. I'll beat you with pistols, not cards, or words."

"No, no," Ace choked out, trying to yank Sam's hand away from his throat. "I'm with you, Sam, whatever you say. All the way."

"Well, that's more like it," Sam said, yanking his hand away from Ace's throat.

He laughed good-naturedly as Ace fell clumsily to the ground, his face red. Ace rubbed at his neck, gasping for air.

Sam sat down again beside the fire. "One of you gents cut off a piece of that meat for me," he said, smiling at each in turn. "And then after my belly is full, we'll head out and find us a pretty little thing named Nicole. Yep, we'll take turns with 'er. How does that sound, gents?"

They all laughed crudely and nodded.

"I have to have her," Sam said as Tom handed him a nice chunk of meat. "I'm going to teach her what it's like to be taken by a true man. I truly won't rest until I have her, the daughter of the man who again shamed me in front of a whole saloon of people by beating me at that game of poker today."

As Sam chewed the meat, its juice rolling from the corners of his mouth, he smiled as he thought about how he had made that idiot gambler pay for what he'd done to Sam Partain.

Yep, he'd made his enemy pay by killing him and his wife and all of the people who'd been ignorant enough to take up residence in the small town of Tyler City.

Now? Once he found Nicole Tyler, he'd amuse himself with her for several days, then kill her.

He waited until all of his men were comfortably full, then stood up quickly and placed his doubled fists on his hips.

"It's time to go and find us a certain pretty lady," Sam said, his voice tight with lust.

He ignored the looks that said none of them wanted to go with him. They knew they must, or be shot.

He owned them all, body and soul.

Chapter Seven

Exhausted, both mentally and physically, Nicole rode onward. At least now she was no longer on flat land where she felt like an easy target for Sam Partain, should he be looking for her.

She still found it hard to believe that her mother and father were dead. If only her father had kept his word about not gambling anymore, perhaps they would still be alive.

Yet when she stopped to think about it, she realized a few hours of poker today could not have caused the fury that must have been festering inside Sam Partain for a long time. His rage was such that he had not settled for killing only the man he obviously hated, but also everyone else that could identify him as the killer.

The whole town of Tyler City was wiped off the map before it was even really known outside the circle of people who lived there.

It gave Nicole the shivers to think that Sam Partain had gone to such lengths to find her father, tracking him to this new town that had sprung up out of nowhere in only a matter of months.

If Sam had been so determined to find her father, would he not be as determined to find her?

She hoped that she was wrong about his continuing need for revenge. She prayed that he was satisfied with having rid the world of the man who had obviously become a thorn in his side long ago.

Her face chapped from the tears she had shed and wiped away so often with the back of her hand, her eyes stinging from crying, Nicole kept riding up the mountain pass she had only recently discovered.

She was so glad there were many miles between herself and the massacre behind her.

Her greatest regret—one that might haunt her the rest of her life—was that she had not felt it was safe enough for her to take the time to bury her parents. She would never forget the sight of them lying there, side by side, their hands clasped together lovingly. In that last moment of their lives, they had reached out for each other, proving just how much they had loved each other.

She knew how much her mother had loved her father. She had stood beside her husband through both good and bad times.

Her mother had scolded her father time and again about his love of poker, and yet she had never threatened to leave him if he would not put that ugly pastime behind him.

He had always reminded his wife that his skill

at gambling was the reason they lived in a fine home and had the best of food. It was the reason his wife had worn the most beautiful clothes and hats, outfits that would compete with those of the richest, best-dressed women in America.

Nicole knew that her mother had been vain, so vain that she had gone along with her husband and his way of making money.

Nicole would never allow herself to be vain. She didn't want a huge home or a closet full of fancy clothes.

She . . . just . . . wanted a life.

She wanted to be a teacher. Even that now might be impossible, if Sam Partain had anything to say about it.

She tried to focus on other things besides the ache in her heart and the fear that plagued her like a toothache that would not go away.

The mountain pass was such a lovely, peaceful place, with water rushing down the mountainside in a waterfall. The sun cast its light into the waterfall, and she could see all the colors of the rainbow twinkling back at her.

But that, too, was a reminder of her mother, of how the diamonds she had worn around her neck and on her fingers always sparkled with the same rainbow colors when the light fell on them.

She just could not seem to get away from reminders of her mother. Even now, she smelled the wondrous scent of roses coming from a vine growing wild up the trunk of a tree. The pink flowers contrasted beautifully with the white bark of the birch tree.

Her mother had always carried the scent of roses with her, for once her husband had won a bottle of French perfume intended for the loser's fiancée.

The frightening howl of a wolf jerked Nicole's mind back to the present, reminding her that she was becoming lost in memories again. She needed to concentrate on her present predicament.

She must be more alert.

She was the only one who could look out for her future. She was alone now.

Totally alone.

She looked in the direction from where she had heard the mournful howling. A shudder went down her spine when she heard it again. This time it sounded like not only one wolf, but two. She could hear them calling from one bluff to another.

And then she had a thought that made her turn icy cold inside.

She remembered that Indians often mimicked animals and birds, using the sounds as signals to each other when they did not want anyone to know they were near.

Could the howls she had heard not been made by an animal at all, but an Indian? Were the Navaho Indians, who were known to live high on this mountain, spying her?

If she went farther, might they suddenly come down from their hideaway and keep her from going nearer their home? Might they kill her?

"I must stop," she whispered, drawing her horse to a sudden halt.

Yes, she was now afraid to go farther, yet at the same time she could not retreat. She felt trapped, like moles back in St. Louis that had been trapped in their underground tunnels when her father put pitchforks down into the ground on both sides of where they were tunneling to impede their further progress.

Nicole had always turned her eyes away when her father had then dug up the blind, furry creatures. She had never known exactly how he had killed them.

Yes, she did feel as though she were in a trap. Would she always be afraid of who might be around the corner waiting for her?

She had gone to school to become a teacher. That was still her goal in life.

It might be the only way to keep her sanity after what she had experienced today.

In the distance, she saw a perfect place to stop. A bluff shadowed the land below it, and a slow, trickling stream was close by.

Yes, she would go on at least that much farther. She would spend the night.

If she felt it was safe enough, she might spend several more days and nights there.

Determined to fight off the fear that had been her companion since she left the scene of her parents' murder, Nicole inhaled a deep, quivering breath, and sank her heels into the flanks of her horse.

She didn't get far before she saw the figure of a man stretched out, asleep, on a blanket. He was lying beside the stream in the shadow of the very bluff that she had chosen for her own campsite.

She wasn't certain what to do.

If there was only one man, she wouldn't feel so terribly threatened. Yet, she reminded herself, it took only one man to kill you.

Should she make a quick retreat before he woke up? Yet if she did, perhaps Sam Partain would be waiting for her when she left the mountain.

So she had to make a choice.

This lone stranger?

Or Sam Partain and his gang?

It did not take much thought to know which she preferred.

This stranger might even help her, whereas she was certain Sam Partain had plans to kill her.

She rode onward, slowly, her eyes never leaving the sleeping form of the man.

She gasped when she was finally able to make out the man's features.

He was an Indian.

He was scantily dressed in a breechclout and moccasins. And his long black hair was spread out beneath his head.

Breathing hard, she stopped her horse. What should she do? Shouldn't she fear Indians far more than Sam Partain?

Yet this was only one Indian. Surely he had traveled alone away from his stronghold for one reason or another.

Her eyes widened then, and she no longer wondered why he was there, all alone. She could see red spots on his body.

And she knew what they were, for she had suffered from the same malady when she was ten years old. Measles.

This Indian had measles.

She recalled how ill she had been with the disease. She had been in bed with a high fever for about three days, and she had been terribly weak.

Because the disease was so contagious, Nicole's mother had put her in a room and let no one enter, not even the servants. When they brought her food, the tray had been set outside her closed bedroom door. After she knew that no one was out in the hallway, she would open the door, take the food and eat what she could, then set what was left back outside in the hallway again.

Apparently, this man had also tried to isolate himself from all others.

She drew rein and dismounted. She secured her horse's reins to a low tree limb, then tiptoed closer to the sleeping Indian.

Now that she was closer than before, she noticed something else about him. Besides the red spots and the flush of fever in his cheeks, she saw how uniquely handsome he was.

She was so taken by his sculpted features, she paused to stare at his face. For a moment she forgot that she should be afraid, that she was in the presence of an Indian.

She had seen many on the riverfront in St. Louis, where they came in their canoes to trade their rich pelts, but she had never been so close to one.

When the Indian suddenly rolled over onto his other side, groaning, Nicole was shaken out of her reverie. Once again she was very aware of his illness.

His back was covered with spots.

He was shivering with fever.

He was a person in need of help.

But she recalled the tales of Indian atrocties she had read about. Wouldn't she be placing herself in mortal danger even by staying there, much less getting closer to him, to offer help?

He rolled again to his other side, so that his face was now facing her, and she gasped in horror when she saw that his eyes were open. He was looking straight at her.

She expected him to leap up and come after her, perhaps use that big, fat knife that rested in a sheath at his right side.

But instead his eyes closed again and he seemed to drift off, perhaps too feverish to have even recognized her as being white.

She started to run back to her horse, but again

his eyes opened and he reached a shaky hand out toward her. Then, to her amazement, he spoke in perfect English.

"Help me," the man gasped, looking at her through fever-bright eyes.

Recalling once again how ill she had been with the measles, and seeing the plea in this warrior's midnight dark eyes, Nicole knew that she could not just leave him there. He was defenseless against roaming forest animals, as well as enemies that might walk on two feet.

She could not help wondering if he had been banished from his village because of his illness. Did his own people not care whether he lived or died?

If that was the case, he had been treated with cruel inhumanity. She felt she must prove to him that not all mankind was heartless and uncaring.

Again she heard the howl of a wolf, surely the very same one she had heard earlier. Again she wondered if it was an Indian, who might be telling others that a white woman had found their sick brother.

Would they sweep down on her and stop her from helping him? She would not doubt that at all.

Today she had witnessed the evil man was capable of.

Those who were white had killed many of their own skin color. Would not men of red skin kill their own if they felt threatened by him?

And they would kill her just as heartlessly.

Ignoring her worst fears, she stepped closer to the Indian. His eyes had closed again. Was he pretending to be asleep, so that he could grab her when she got close enough?

Or was he truly asleep again, the illness robbing him of his strength, as it did when she had had the same disease?

Her heart pounded as she stepped even closer to him. She stopped just a heartbeat away from him and gazed down.

She now realized that he was probably in his mid or late twenties, with a body that most any white man would kill for.

Such muscles, such smooth skin, oh, so much of everything that awoke feelings within Nicole she never knew existed!

She had to forget all that for the time being and do what she could to help him. She just hoped that her attempt to be a Good Samaritan would not end in her own death.

She ripped a portion of her cotton petticoat away and took it to the stream to wet it.

She returned to where the Indian still lay so quietly on the blanket. She wondered if she had lost her sanity, getting so close to an Indian, who could kill her with one plunge of his powerful knife.

She saw where he had put down his quiver of arrows, and then looked at the lovely bow that rested not far from where he lay.

Now that she looked around her, she saw his horse tethered amongst some nearby trees. On it was a buckskin bag that must hold more of his belongings. She also saw a rifle in the gun boot.

Frightened at the sight of the weapons, Nicole swallowed hard and fell to her knees beside him.

Gently, she applied the wet rag to his fevered brow. As she wiped it, his eyes flew open and one of his hands reached up and grabbed her wrist.

She gasped as she felt the true strength of the hand that held her wrist. Had he tricked her into coming near just so he could grab her?

Their eyes met in silent battle.

Chapter Eight

It was the habit of the Mormon people to come together in one place to eat their meals. The sun poured warmly through the dining hall window and upon the long table around that sat the adults of the new Mormon settlement of Hope. The children sat at another table of their own, a little distance from their parents.

They spoke quietly among themselves as they ate their dinner of fried chicken. The milk in their tin cups came from the cows that were housed in a barn at the far end of the village. In other smaller buildings, hogs and chickens were kept.

All of the animals, including the horses that were kept in a corral beside the barn, were owned communally, with no one having more than another. Earlier in the day, the young men of the village had cared for the horses and other animals, while the girls had busied themselves gathering eggs.

The little ones had amused themselves holding the new golden chicks, or petting the foals.

Other children had fed the hogs from the food that had not been eaten the prior day. It made a fine meal for the animals that were being fattened for butchering in the near future.

Jeremiah and his family were the newest addition to the small town of Hope, welcomed warmly with hugs and gifts, and even a small house already built and ready for them to move into. It was not a cabin, but a whitewashed house made of planks of wood, like the other houses in the community.

It had rooms enough so that the girls could sleep separate from their mothers, and a well-equipped kitchen. There was even a water pump installed at the sink.

Happy to finally be in the new settlement, Jeremiah ate his chicken heartily as he sat straight and tall in his chair, with a wife on each side of him.

He glanced over his shoulder at the children, all sitting together, and noticed that the oldest of the boys were teasing the girls who sat opposite them at the table.

Jeremiah smiled at how well his daughters took to the teasing, for he knew that among those fine young men might be the very ones who would be Jeremiah's sons-in-law one of these days.

He returned to his eating, thinking about how good it was to have finally arrived at Hope, where his family could live with others who shared their beliefs.

He would make certain that his family was happy in this community.

And now that they were all settled down, he had decided to find himself a third wife from among the unmarried daughters of his friends.

He wanted many children, and he hungered for a son.

Children were the future of the Mormon people. The more children born into each family, the more blessings would be bestowed upon them.

He had not admitted to anyone his embarrassment at not having sons, but he felt it made him look less of a man in the eyes of the others. But he was embarrassed. If it took five more wives to bring him a son, so be it!

A commotion outside the dining hall drew his attention to the door. Someone had just galloped up on horseback.

No one needed to get up to see who had arrived, for the man burst through the door, breathless. He strode over to the dining table, alarm showing in his dark eyes.

It was Jacob, the one chosen to keep watch for marauding Indians and others who might mean harm to the community. His beard was golden and his eyes blue, his clothes covered with dust from his hasty ride. He wrung his hands as he looked from man to man and then finally spoke.

His voice quivered, betraying just how distraught he was over the news he was bringing.

"There's been a massacre," Jacob blurted out. "I came upon it when I rode to Tyler City to see how our new neighbors were faring. I didn't have to get close to see the black smoke billowing into the sky. I knew from that smoke that there was some disaster."

"Tell us about it," one of the elders commanded. "You said a massacre. Does that mean that no one in that new town survived?"

"No one," Jacob gulped out as he wiped a tear from the corner of his eye. "I came upon the scene not long after it happened, for some of the buildings were still afire, while others lay in smoldering ash."

For several moments, Jeremiah's mind was absorbed by the horrors of Jacob's report, but, then he suddenly remembered the young and beautiful woman on the stagecoach, whose destination had been Tyler City.

She was headed there to join her family. She had spoken of being the teacher for the new community.

He got a sick feeling in the pit of his stomach as he wondered if she had arrived in the town before or after the massacre.

Without further thought, he jumped up from his chair. He moved so quickly that it fell over on its back on the floor, which drew all eyes his way.

"I have something that must be done," Jeremiah stiffly announced. "Which of you men wants to join me?"

"What are you going to do?" one of the men asked as he stood up and gazed at him. "Why now?"

Jeremiah did not want his wives to know what he had on his mind—the welfare of the pretty woman from the stagecoach—so he did not even give them a glance as he stepped away from the table.

"Those of you who want to join me, come outside and I shall explain my plan to you," Jeremiah said brusquely. "But I only need a few. The rest should stay behind and protect our women and children. Who is to say whether our community might be the next to be killed off?"

The women gasped at that statement, and some of the smallest children began to cry.

"We must face reality," Jeremiah said, sorry to see that what he had said had upset the women and children. "There are those who do not enjoy seeing a prosperous community. They are the sort who do not know how to be successful themselves. It is that kind who kills without feeling. It is that kind we must protect ourselves from."

He looked around at the men. "Come now, those who will ride with me today," he said tightly. "Come outside and I will tell you my plan."

Jeremiah led the way as those who would ride with him followed.

The others stayed behind in the dining hall, already discussing amongst themselves what they must do to protect their wives and children.

Outside the dining hall, out of earshot of his two wives, Jeremiah gathered the men around him. "On our way to Hope, there was a woman in the stagecoach," he said, moving his eyes slowly from man to man. "Her destination was Tyler City. In fact, the town was named after her family. She was a fragile-appearing woman who would not be able to fend for herself alone in the world. You know that no lady, especially one as tiny and fragile in appearance as that young woman, can survive, alone. Think about your wives. Should they be parted from you, do you think they would have the skills to survive?"

Each man shook his head.

"And so do you agree that we must go to rescue this young lady, who may be out there alone, afraid, and helpless?" Jeremiah asked, not giving even a hint of the true reason that he wanted to find her.

Although she was petite, the girl had not truly looked fragile in any other way. He was just saying that in order to make the men feel sorry for her enough to go and seek her out.

The very moment she had stepped into the coach, he had been attracted to her. He had seen her as someone who would make him the perfect third wife.

She was so young and healthy, surely she could bear him a son . . . perhaps many!

He just hoped and prayed that she was still alive and that he and his friends could find her. If they did, they would invite her to return to Hope with them.

Although Jeremiah's true need of her was to bear him sons, he would tell her that she was welcome in their town, and that she could use her skills as a teacher, instructing the children.

Thus far, no teachers had agreed to come to Hope.

If this woman, whose name he now recalled was Nicole, was rescued, wouldn't she be more than willing to remain in Hope as their teacher, and then . . . later . . . become a wife to one of the community's most upstanding citizens?

After the men agreed that Nicole was worth looking for and saving, they readied themselves with firearms and then went to the corral for their horses.

Jeremiah felt eyes on him as he rode from the town. He turned and saw his two wives standing at the edge of Hope, hand in hand, watching as he rode out, possibly to his death.

He had thought of that, himself, but each man was well equipped now with a rifle in his gun boot or at the side of his horses. He had plenty of backup.

They also had said a silent prayer before mounting their steeds.

Jeremiah looked away from his wives and gazed straight ahead again, hoping by nightfall he would be still alive, and that he would have saved a woman whom he already thought of as his.

Chapter Nine

Her heart pounding hard, her breath now coming in short, frightened gulps, Nicole felt glued to the spot as she recalled the last few minutes.

"Leave," the Indian had commanded, gazing into her eyes while he gripped her wrist. "Go away. Leave now, or you will die."

Nicole's pulse had raced at that spoken threat.

She'd looked quickly at his rifle, which was too far for him to reach. Then her eyes had settled on the knife that was sheathed at his waist. Again she'd looked at his eyes. Slowly, they had closed, and his grip on her wrist had lessened until finally his hand fell away.

She knew that she should take this opportunity to jump up, mount her horse and ride away, but as she saw it, he was no threat at all to her. Although his grip on her wrist had been strong enough, she still didn't believe that he had the strength it would take to harm her.

Although his words seemed to ring in her ears and linger there, Nicole couldn't just leave without at least trying to help him.

How could she turn her back on someone who was in need of help, even if that person was an Indian? And hadn't he pleaded earlier for her help?

She couldn't make any sense of his contradictory words.

But she was very aware that measles could be fatal. Most people recovered from the illness, yet some didn't.

She knew that there was no cure for the disease. Tender, loving care from a loved one was often what helped the ill pull through. Her mother's loving care had brought her through the disease.

This man seemed to have no one.

Had his own people chased him off, from fear of getting measles themselves?

He was apparently a man all alone and she just could not leave him there without at least trying to help lower his temperature. She believed that if someone did die from measles, it was because of a fever that had gotten out of control. And that seemed to be the case with this Indian.

No matter what he said, she would take the time to bathe his brow and his powerful chest with cool water. Even if it took her all night, she would try to help him in the only way she knew how.

She was in no hurry to leave this place. At least here she would be safe from Sam Partain.

She would not allow herself to think about that, not now, not when she had the chance to save somebody's life as she had not had the chance to save her own parents.

Nicole gazed again at the sleeping Indian.

Yes, she was in no hurry to get anywhere, for she had no destination. She had no place to go and was as alone as the Indian; time meant nothing to her anymore.

Her future was one large question mark.

When Nicole heard the Indian groan, she rushed to the stream and wet the piece of her petticoat again, but didn't wring it out. She wanted to get back to the Indian with as much water on the cloth as she could.

With the cloth dripping wet, she hurried to him, then quickly knelt and applied it to his feverish brow, his cheeks, and then his chest.

Suddenly Nicole felt the Indian shiver, whether in pleasure or shock at the cold water. She did not know.

She looked quickly at his eyes and grew pale when she found them open again. He was watching her every move.

She flinched, dropped the cloth, and crawled quickly away, stopping a few feet from him. Only then did she turn to look at him again.

When their gazes met and held, Nicole felt a strange reaction, like a butterfly fluttering inside her belly.

The Indian continued to gaze into her eyes, as though he was looking far into her soul. His look gave her a sudden, strange feeling of sensuality at the juncture of her thighs. She had never experienced such feelings before.

It was an awakening of sorts, and it felt strangely delicious.

Nicole wondered if these feelings were how a woman felt when she became attracted to a man. Up to now, her life had been too full with family and schooling responsibilities for her to consider having a man in her life.

And she shouldn't consider it now, especially not with this man. He was a redskin, an enemy to all whites.

But how could she deny how marvelously handsome this Indian was, even while lying there so ill?

He had such a beautifully sculpted face.

And his eyes.

Ah, how his eyes seemed to hypnotize her. They were so dark and penetrating, so beautiful.

And then she could not help looking at his powerful chest and muscled arms, shoulders, and even his legs.

She had never seen a man nude, not even her father, so she could not compare his body with others. But it did not take comparison for Nicole to know that this man was a perfect example of masculine beauty.

She had to remind herself all over again that this was not just any man. He was an Indian. He was someone who was forbidden to her because his skin was copper and hers was white.

But it was as though this man had her in some

sort of mystical grip. He did not even need to hold her by the wrist anymore to keep her by his side.

It was in the way his eyes spoke to her when she gazed into them.

She had never allowed a man to look so deeply into her eyes, or . . . at . . . her! She always fled anyone who seemed unusually interested in her.

Yet, strangely enough, she still knelt there, strangely hypnotized by the Indian.

Eagle Wolf was not too ill to realize that he was powerfully attracted to this beautiful, petite, fiery-haired woman.

Her skin was white, but her heart was golden, for she must know the danger of being so close to an Indian. He was sure she'd heard many tales about how devilish all Indians were.

Yet there she was, risking everything in order to help him. He saw her as very courageous, and he was touched deeply by her kindness.

But he felt that he was duty-bound to warn her that not all Indians were as peaceful as he.

His people had suffered much at the hands of whites. It would matter not to most Indians that she was a delicate woman. All they would see about her was that she was white, an enemy.

Many warriors would enjoy raping, then killing her, even taking her fiery red scalp to flaunt on a scalp pole.

He had no such scalp pole. Nor did any other warrior of his Owl Clan.

They were decent in everything they did. And they would never murder and then rape any woman.

"You did not flee from this man with red skin," Eagle Wolf said, his eyes searching hers. "You have helped this man who most whites see as an enemy. You have helped this Indian although you know the danger? Today, white woman, the danger is twofold for you. I have the killing disease that has been brought to Indian country by your people, and I am a man with red skin. Do you not fear both?"

"I do not know much about Indians," Nicole said softly, finding it oh, so strange to actually be talking with an Indian.

Yet there she was and there he was.

"All that I know of your people is what I have read in books," Nicole said. "And as for the disease that has downed you? Few die from measles. I doubt that you will, either."

"You call this sickness by the strange name measles?" Eagle Wolf said, arching an eyebrow. "I am not familiar with . . . measles. I have the deadly disease that is known by the name smallpox."

Nicole's eyes widened. "You think you have smallpox?" she asked, her gaze moving from red spot to red spot on his chest.

"Is that not what it is called?" Eagle Wolf asked, again searching her eyes.

"No. What you have is not smallpox," Nicole said, certain she was right.

"What is this thing you call measles?" he asked, gazing intently into her grass green eyes.

"The red spots on your body prove that you have measles; the marks of smallpox look very different," Nicole murmured.

She was surprised that he knew the English language so well.

"My people were told about the white man bringing the disease called smallpox to our country, sometimes purposely in order to kill off entire clans," Eagle Wolf said dryly. "My wife died from the same disease that caused the red spots on my body. If this is named measles, then measles killed my wife. I, too, will surely die, and so will you."

"I know that I will not have measles again by coming in contact with you," Nicole replied. "You cannot have measles more than once. I had it. And I am very sorry about your wife. Some do die from measles, but not many. The fever is surely what claimed her. Did your wife's temperature go very high?"

"Very," Eagle Wolf said solemnly, slowly nodding. "Nothing could stop it. Not even our people's shaman, who is skilled at healing."

Nicole recalled earlier how he had grabbed her by the wrist and said that she would die. "Earlier you told me to leave, that I was going to die," she said. "Did you say that to me because of your concern that I would get the same disease as you? Did you also believe that you were going to die?"

"My wife died, so, *ho*, yes, I expected to also," Eagle Wolf said. "I felt that I needed to warn you."

Nicole remembered how frightened she had felt at that moment, and was so glad to know now that he had not meant he would kill her, himself, if she stayed there.

She truly felt as though she could relax now, and continue offering him help without fearing that in the end his thank-you would be to kill her.

"Will you allow me to continue helping you?" she asked. "I can stay with you long enough to bring down your fever by bathing your skin with cool water from the stream. I can even feed you, so that you can regain your strength and return to your people a strong, well man."

"Why would you do this for me?" Eagle Wolf asked, more amazed by this woman as each moment passed. "I a Navaho and most whites would call me a savage."

"You are a human being," Nicole said softly. "I do not judge people by their skin color. My parents taught me differently."

"Where are your parents?" Eagle Wolf asked. "Why are you traveling alone? Why are you not with them?"

She didn't think she could bear to talk about how she had found her parents. The pain of speaking about it would be almost the same as being there again.

Instead of answering him, she asked a question of her own. "Are you strong enough to move closer to the stream?" she blurted out. "It will be more convenient for me as I bathe your feverish brow with cool water. The water will help bring down the fever."

Again touched deeply by her kindness, he nodded. With Nicole's help, he stumbled to the stream, then collapsed in a dead faint beside it.

Nicole gasped at just how weak he was; his fainting was proof of that. She hoped that she wasn't too late to help him.

She believed this man was not to be feared, but admired. There was something majestic about him, as though he might be more than a mere warrior.

He had the demeanor of a mighty chief.

As she slowly bathed his face, her eyes were drawn again to admire his handsomeness. She relived how his voice had sounded, so deep, so masculine, and so kind.

As she continued to bathe his hot flesh, she prayed that the treatment would work. She would hate to see such a man as he die!

Her jaws tightened in determination, vowing to herself that she would not let him die.

She wondered about this wife who had died. Had she been so beautiful that he could not see beauty in another woman?

Could he ever care for a woman whose skin was white?

Knowing how foolish she was to allow herself such fantasies, Nicole forced her thoughts elsewhere as she continued to bathe his body.

The future. What did it hold for her? Where could she go when she felt it was safe enough to wander from this mountain?

She truly did not want to return to St. Louis and live with her aunt Dot and uncle Zeb. She had felt stifled there.

So then . . . where could she go?

Who else but them could she turn to?

She again gazed at the Indian. She could not deny that she was drawn to him. He had awakened feelings within her that she had not known existed, and she knew that was because he was a man who had made her feel like a woman.

Chapter Ten

As the setting sun painted an orange glow on the mountain, and the birds called to each other as they settled into their nests for the night, Nicole was feeling a loneliness she had never known before. This would be her first night of having no parents.

As dusk fell, Nicole hugged herself.

When Eagle Wolf groaned softly in his sleep near the campfire she had managed to build, she looked down at him.

Before he had drifted off to sleep again, Eagle Wolf had told her how to build the fire. She had never had a reason to know how before now.

After she had gotten the rest of the campsite ready for the long night ahead, she had pulled her own blanket from her travel bag, and a shawl, which she'd wrapped around her shoulders to ward off the chill she felt as fog drifted in on all sides of her.

Starved, Nicole had found berries enough to fill her emptiness until she got the courage to hunt something more substantial. But not until morning.

She did not dare wander from this place in the dark. Nicole had no doubt that mountain lions were aplenty. And once again, she only now heard the frightening call of a wolf.

She peered up at the moon, which had now replaced the sun in the sky. She shivered at how ghostly it looked as it shone through the fog. She scooted to the edge of her blanket, closer to the fire, then looked over her shoulder when she heard crickets begin their nightly song.

As a child, she had listened to them from her bed. She had always loved their chirping. Even when she was a child, they had brought peace to her heart.

When she thought of them now, she recalled the time when she had decided to call the song of the crickets "night music."

She felt a growing inner peace even now as she listened to another familiar night sound that she had heard while in her home on the shores of the Mississippi just outside the bustling city of St. Louis. An owl was hooting in the dark.

When she saw fireflies with their flashing lanterns begin to rise from the grass all around her, tears came to her eyes. She thought about the times she had gone outside on early evenings with her mother and played amid the fireflies, giggling when one landed on her arm.

Those were such innocent, wonderful, happy times. She would never know them again, unless she had her own child one day to share such things with.

She had never thought about children of her own before, but now, strangely enough, she did.

She hated to believe that she would remain so alone in the world all of her life. Now she longed to find a man she could share her life with.

"Your name?"

It was almost eerie the way that male voice interrupted her thoughts of finding a man to share her life with. It was as though her thoughts had carried to Eagle Wolf, awakening him.

She blushed and then gasped softly when she saw that he was moving to a sitting position.

His face was no longer flushed, and his eyes were clear. Both things surely meant that his fever was gone.

His warm, wondrous smile, and his voice as he again spoke to her, made Nicole's heart skip a beat. Her reaction confirmed just how attracted she was to him.

"What is your name?" Eagle Wolf asked again, wondering why asking her such a simple question should bring color to her cheeks in a blush.

He had been too ill earlier to even think about her name, much less ask it.

But now?

Something inside himself, beyond mere curiosity, made him want to know more about her.

He brushed aside the fact that she was white.
She was like no white person he had ever known.

She was generous and kind. She was absolutely
beautiful, both outside and in.

It was because of her that he was beginning to
feel like himself again, instead of an injured animal, at the mercy of any who might come across
him while he was ill and alone.

"Nicole," she murmured. "Nicole Tyler."

"How is it that you are not afraid of Eagle
Wolf?" he asked.

"When I first saw you, I must admit that I was
afraid," Nicole said softly. "But then I realized
you were ill. I hoped to help you, and I believe
that I have."

She paused, then said, "I have, haven't I? You
do look as though you are feeling better. I don't
believe you have a temperature any longer."

Eagle Wolf smiled over the fire at her. "*Ho*, it is
gone," he said, slowly nodding. He laughed softly
and good-naturedly. "Eagle Wolf sees you now as
a white shaman."

Again Nicole blushed, for she knew that Eagle
Wolf was teasing her.

"Why are you traveling alone?" Eagle Wolf
suddenly asked.

The question unnerved Nicole. She had not
been able to tell him about her parents earlier.
Could she do it now?

If so, would the burden of the pain and sorrow she was carrying in her heart be lessened?

And was this man the right one to tell such a thing to?

Yet it did seem so right to talk to him and even share her grief with him.

She had never met a man who seemed so sincerely kind and caring. Surely it was because she had been the same to him.

"It was not my intention to be alone," Nicole finally blurted out, lowering her eyes so that he would not see the wetness of tears as she fought the urge to cry.

"Then why is that you are?" Eagle Wolf asked, lifting an eyebrow. "Surely you know the risks for a woman traveling alone in this land where so much danger is present."

"Yes, I truly know the danger," Nicole said, slowly raising her eyes, so that she could look into his. She swallowed hard. "I now know it much better than most people would."

"Do you mean that you are in danger with me, because I am an Indian?" Eagle Wolf asked, hoping that his assumption was wrong. He had not wanted to put fear in her heart, but trust.

"Oh, no," Nicole quickly said. "Certainly not. You have given me no reason to be afraid."

"Then what did you mean?" Eagle Wolf asked, now truly curious.

Then a sudden remembrance came to him. He recalled seeing this woman riding toward the burning town called Tyler City. He had not yet asked her the purpose of her journey.

And then he recalled her last name.

Tyler!

The name of the town that had burned had been Tyler City. Was she associated with that town somehow?

"You seem hesitant to answer me," Eagle Wolf said. "I saw you riding toward Tyler City as it burned. Your last name is Tyler. Did you have family there?"

That question stunned Nicole into silence.

He had seen her even before she had found him on the mountain. He had actually seen her riding toward Tyler City. She was sure he had guessed who her father was.

Did that mean that he knew her father by reputation? Did he know him as a gambler, known for cheating while playing poker?

She inhaled nervously, for she was suddenly awakened to just how widespread her father's reputation might be. Would his shame now follow her around for the rest of her life whenever she was asked her last name?

At this moment she could not help resenting her father as much as she mourned him. He was at peace in death, while she would never know who might point an accusing finger at her because of who her father had been.

She would have to live with his bad reputation forever.

"I see that my question has made you uncomfortable," Eagle Wolf said. "I can understand why.

Surely upon your arrival in Tyler City you saw the worst thing possible for a daughter. Surely your parents did not live?"

"No, they didn't, and I truly do not wish to talk about it," Nicole murmured, slowly looking up into his dark eyes. "It causes such pain in my heart even to think about it, much less . . . talk about it," she said softly.

"I do understand," Eagle Wolf said thickly. "I, too, have lost those I loved. I have told you that my wife died from measles. I also lost my father and mother." Eagle Wolf gazed sadly into the dancing flames of the fire. "It is now only myself and my brother . . ."

He stopped at that, guessing that she did not even have a sibling to share her grief. In life, there were so many things that could cause heartache, but one must learn go on living.

The same philosophy applied to him. Although he had recently lost his wife, he could not help noticing the beauty of this woman, Nicole. Should it be the will of the Great Spirit that he love this woman, and that she love him, then so be it.

But it was too soon, just now, to think about such possibilities. Their relationship was too new to consider being in love.

He must never forget that being a chief required many things of him. He must use utmost care choosing a woman to bring into the Owl Clan as his future wife.

"I am suddenly hungry," Eagle Wolf said, glad

that he had found a way to break through the awkward silence that had fallen between himself and Nicole.

He nodded toward his tethered horse and the parfleche bag that still hung at its right side. "My bag is on my horse," he said. "In it is food that I packed for my journey. It is called pemmican. I would share it with you tonight if you can get it for us."

Nicole was so glad that all talk of her parents, especially her father and how they had died, was forgotten by Eagle Wolf.

He had surely seen the hurt that it had brought to her heart, and understood. He, too, had recently lost loved ones.

She hurried to his bag and opened it. After searching through it, she found what she guessed must be the pemmican he had spoken about.

It was wrapped in a thin strip of buckskin.

She took it back to him.

He unwrapped the buckskin and tore the meat into two equal pieces, giving Nicole one. She chose to sit beside him, rather than across the fire from him.

They ate in silence for a moment, then Eagle Wolf began talking again about his wife.

"My wife Precious Stone and I were not married for long," he said sadly. "It was a marriage of convenience only. I wanted children, for children are the future of our people. My clan has been depleted by wars with our enemy, the Ute, and with the United States government. Finally, I led my people to safety, to a place where no white men dare go. There my people will prosper again."

"You said that you led your people to safety," Nicole murmured, trying to sort through this information he had suddenly revealed to her. She was surprised that he would be so open with her, especially about a wife he had not really loved.

"I am chief of the Owl Clan of Navaho," Eagle Wolf proudly stated. He noticed that her eyes widened in wonder.

"I did not know," Nicole said softly. She didn't tell him that she had guessed he might be a leader of his people.

A chief! She was in the presence of a powerful Navaho chief.

Yes, she was impressed.

"When my father died at the hands of the white man's cavalry, I was named chief after him. After the battle was ended and our people were victorious over the white-eyed soldiers, I took them to safety on this mountain and here we shall remain," Eagle Wolf said thickly.

Nicole knew, from his description of the battle, how he had fought and won, that he must have killed many white men. But she couldn't fault him for that. Eagle Wolf's father had most likely died right before his eyes, shot by a soldier who saw Indians as nothing but savages.

No, she did not blame him for fighting for his people's survival.

She had always thought it wrong that the white man had taken everything from the Indians. She knew the government was still trying to make certain all Indians were rounded up and placed on reservations.

It was disgraceful, and she was ashamed to say she was part of a nation that had wronged the Indians so badly.

"Tell me about yourself," Eagle Wolf said. "But only what you are comfortable telling."

"I love children," Nicole said, then found her cheeks burning suddenly with a blush when she remembered that he had just spoken about children being the future of his people. She hoped he wouldn't think she had said that to impress him. She had only meant to tell him about wanting to be a teacher.

"I went to school and received my teaching credentials," Nicole blurted out. "It was my deep desire to teach children, for I do love them so much."

At her words, a new thought came to Eagle Wolf, but he decided not to voice it aloud. If Nicole loved teaching children so much, could she not teach Navaho children what she had learned to teach white?

His people's children could learn the ways of white people so that they could avoid their tricks.

But the presence of one white person in his stronghold could lead to others discovering it. No matter how he was attracted to this woman, he could not chance taking her to his home.

Nicole suddenly realized just how weary she was from the long day she had just gone through. "I am so tired," she said softly. "I must retire for the night. Will you be all right while I sleep?"

She glanced hesitantly at his weapons. Was she being foolish to trust that he would not kill her as she slept?

Eagle Wolf noticed Nicole looking at his weapons.

Although he thought she did not see him as her enemy, he understood her hesitance.

"Do not be afraid to sleep," Eagle Wolf reassured her as he reached out and gently took one of her hands in his. "White woman, I understand why you might still be afraid to trust me, for it is rare that white people trust men with red skin. I assure you that you are safe while you are with me. When I look at you, I do not see the color of your skin, but the kindness of your heart."

He gently squeezed her hand. He saw that his words caused a flush to rise to Nicole's cheeks. She now looked trustingly into his eyes.

"I thank you for what you have done for me," he said, then slowly eased his hand from hers.

He nodded over the fire toward her blanket, then again gazed into her eyes.

"Go now," he softly encouraged. "Sleep in peace. I shall do the same. Tomorrow is another day, but tonight we must rest."

Nicole smiled sweetly at him, then rose and walked over to where she had spread the blanket for herself earlier. She stretched out on the blanket, sighed, and was soon fast asleep.

Chapter Eleven

The moon scarcely showed through the smoke that continued to rise from the burned town of Tyler City. As Jeremiah and his friends rode toward the grayish haze that lay heavy in the air, he knew that he had found the city that had been erased from the map in a single day.

As Jeremiah rode into what remained of the city, his horse's hooves scattered ash on both sides of him. He gasped as his lungs were filled with the stench of burning wood and death.

His eyes filled with tears as he looked from body to body. The glow of the moon pushed its way through the ash-filled air, showing Jeremiah and his friends just how horrendously the people of this new little town had died.

They had not had a chance against those who had come with hate in their hearts. Not a soul had been spared. He mourned for these people who had surely risen from their beds for a new day this morning with hope and love, and dreams of tomorrow.

Then Jeremiah recalled his purpose in coming

to this horrific scene of death in the first place. For a moment the lovely woman had been forgotten in his horror at the bodies lying on the ground all around him.

"Nicole Tyler," he whispered to himself as he glanced over at a sign bearing the name Tyler City, which had somehow made it through the devastation intact.

Yes, this had been Nicole's destination. He had found out that much about her during their time together in the stagecoach. She had planned to join her parents there and become this small community's schoolteacher.

"A community bearing her family's name, no less," he said, looking over at Jacob, who sat on his horse beside Jeremiah. "Jacob, it seems there were no survivors."

"Unless those who did survive managed to escape without being seen," Jacob said, wiping at his mouth with the back of his hand. "Lord a'mighty, Jeremiah, who could be so evil? How could anyone hate so much that they had no mercy on anyone?"

Jeremiah swallowed down vomit as he again looked slowly around him. "It's certain there are no survivors here," he said hoarsely. "But still, perhaps some escaped the wrath of those madmen. Perhaps Nicole arrived here after the massacre was over and then fled for her life, fearing the killers might find her there, alone."

"They might even now still be near and see us

gawking at what they left behind," Jacob said, fear in his eyes and voice. "Jeremiah, we'd best head back for home. What if those who did this go to our little community and do the same? Lord a'mighty, Jeremiah, they might be there even now. Our women and children . . ."

"Do not borrow trouble, Jacob," Jeremiah said. "I believe the killers are far, far away now, avoiding being caught by the cavalry. Isn't there a fort anywhere near here?"

"No. If there were, the cavalry would be here now, burying the dead," Jacob said tightly.

"As it is, that chore has been left to us, for there is no way that I could ever rest again without knowing that we did the right thing," Jeremiah said.

"But, Jeremiah, the risk we would be taking by taking time to bury the dead is too great. Surely it's not worth losing our own lives," Jacob argued. "We have our wives and children to consider. Let's go home, Jeremiah. Let's go home now."

Jeremiah ignored Jacob's whining as he dismounted. He was so glad that the others who had come with them had not spoken out. They just sat on their horses, stunned and quiet.

"Come on," Jeremiah said, looking from man to man. "There has to be a shovel somewhere. Maybe even more than one. We must start digging graves. Now!"

The men dismounted and secured their horses' reins to a hitching rail that stood some distance away from the burned buildings. They found three shovels in the ashes and started digging graves beneath the moonlight.

"I wonder if Nicole arrived here just in time to be killed with the others?" Jeremiah worried aloud, ignoring Jacob's frown.

Jeremiah laid his shovel aside, and fighting the urge to vomit again, he went to the first person that would be placed in the shallow grave he had managed to dig.

He swallowed hard, then grabbed the man by what was left of his wrists. He dragged the body over and rolled it into the grave. The other men followed suit.

"Indians sure didn't do this," Jeremiah said to Jacob as they each began digging another grave, side by side. "There were no arrows. That surely means this was done by white men, but what I don't understand is how could white men hate other white people so much that they would kill them so heartlessly? Why would they do this? We Mormons teach love, not hate."

"Jeremiah, you know as well as I that there is much hate in this world," Jacob said, stopping to rest a moment as he leaned against his shovel. "It is not something that anyone can ever figure out. Let's just get this done and return home to those we love. We can't let anything like this happen to our peaceful little community."

"Yes, you're right," Jeremiah said, stopping his digging when the grave was deep enough. He dreaded with every fiber of his being having to drag another body over to it. "Jacob, surely Nicole Tyler is still alive somewhere, for I don't see her body here."

"Unless she is one of those that can't be identified because of how badly they are burned," Jacob suggested softly.

"Yes, perhaps," Jeremiah said. He sighed heavily. "But something deep inside tells me that she is still alive, somewhere."

They all continued burying the dead until none were left to bury.

A quiet prayer was said over the graves, and then Jeremiah and his friends mounted their horses and headed back toward their homes.

Jeremiah knew now that he must forget the woman. Since he hadn't found her body among the others, she could be anywhere, with anyone.

His duties awaited him back at the settlement. It just wasn't meant for Nicole Tyler to be his third wife, and that was that.

Chapter Twelve

Although there was only a crescent moon on this second night that Nicole was with Eagle Wolf, it lighted the heavens and all that lay beneath. The sky was filled with a brilliant scattering of stars, twinkling brightly.

Every now and then the campfire Nicole and Eagle Wolf were sitting beside sent sparks into the air, looking like orange fireflies against the dark sky.

Nothing seemed real, though, to Nicole. Her life had changed so much in such a short period of time.

Was it truly only a few days ago that she was in St. Louis, content, with a bright future ahead of her?

How excited she'd been as she packed her belongings so that she could finally be with her parents again. It had been hard staying behind in St. Louis, until she had that teaching degree in her hand.

She had that degree now, but everything else she loved was gone from her.

Of course she still had her aunt Dot and uncle Zeb, who would welcome her back with open arms should she decide to return to St. Louis. But she had been very aware that their health was quickly failing.

In fact, they were not well enough to hear about what had happened to Nicole's mother and father. Knowing such a thing would surely kill them.

Nicole decided she could not let them know about the tragedy in their family. St. Louis and their home could not be her destination.

If she returned there, her aunt and uncle would want to know why, and she couldn't reveal the truth.

No, she would never tell them about the horrors of how her parents had died. She could hardly bear knowing it herself.

As she had slept last night, the scene of death that she had found at Tyler City came back to haunt her dreams.

Perhaps if she had been able to bury her parents, she might be able to sleep at night. But she hadn't buried them, and she was afraid, still, to go near the town.

It was truly a ghost town now, with none but the dead to inhabit it.

Those who had lived there were merchants and their families who had been encouraged by her father to join in this new venture with him. Only months ago they'd built their establishments and their homes. They had decided to follow her father because they thought they were going to be part of a growing, prospering city. As they feverishly tried to reach their families when the shooting began, had they had the time to realize how disastrous that decision was?

Had any of them been able to be with their loved ones when they were killed? Or had they died apart, never to see or hold one another again?

"Is the rabbit cooked well enough for you?"

The deep voice of the man she was so attracted to now broke through Nicole's thoughts.

The day they had just spent together had been a little awkward. Both of them seemed to realize that they had feelings for each other, but both realized that carrying their feelings further was an impossible dream.

Nicole knew that Eagle Wolf's people had cause to hate all whites, as did Eagle Wolf, himself. She would never be accepted by them.

Nevertheless, she had oh, so enjoyed these moments with him. Today, his fever was gone and he had been strong enough to hunt for their supper.

He had supplied the rabbit meat and she had supplied a pocketful of delicious berries that she had found while he had been on the hunt.

This evening meal with him would be cherished in her memory forever, for even though she had not told him, she knew it must be their last time to eat together.

Yes, tonight, after he fell asleep, she would sneak away and leave him to return to his normal life.

He had told her today, as they had talked eagerly, that he was well enough now to return to his people. He did not want to worry them unnecessarily.

His temperature was gone and the red spots were fading on his skin.

Yes, he had fought and won the battle with measles. He was free to return home and resume his duties as chief.

He had even confided in Nicole that he had not felt completely comfortable leaving his younger brother in charge.

He knew that his brother was power-hungry and would cherish these moments of leadership. He might enjoy them so much that he would wish to remain the Owl Clan's chief.

Those words made Nicole shiver. Would his brother want Eagle Wolf out of his life permanently?

"The meat is delicious," Nicole finally blurted out, having found herself once again immersed in disturbing thoughts.

But that had been the way the latter part of the day had been as they both tried to accept the fact that the instant attraction between them could lead nowhere.

They had not yet talked about how they would say good-bye and mean it.

She had decided that farewells would be too painful. After Eagle Wolf went to bed tonight, she would only pretend to fall asleep. She would slip away into the night while he lay asleep, thinking she would be there in the morning when he awakened.

"You have been so quiet," Eagle Wolf said, searching Nicole's eyes. "Even more so than usual. What have you been thinking about so hard?"

"Things I shouldn't," Nicole said, hoping he would suppose that she meant the massacre.

Oh, how could she leave?

Did she have the courage to sneak away into the night, feeling that she was leaving someone who might be her soul mate?

She believed she was born to be with him. It was obvious how they felt about each other as they talked and as they looked deeply into each other's eyes. If one of them accidentally brushed a hand against the flesh of the other, it was as though they had touched heaven!

"You will never be able to forget what happened to your parents," Eagle Wolf said, leaning toward the fire and dropping a bone into its flames. "But the memories will become less hurtful as time goes on."

He relaxed again beside the fire, his stomach full. "In my time, I have seen too many die who should still be living and enjoying their families," he continued. "It never gets easier to witness death. But eventually some peace enters your heart so that you can go on with your life. My people's Great Spirit has always helped us through heartache, and given us the strength to accept that which caused the heartache. In time, you will think about your parents and only remember the good, not the bad. When you see them in your dreams, or your mind's eye, you will see them smiling back at you. Know, always, they are with you even when you cannot see them."

He placed a hand over his heart. "It is here, in your heart, that they will always remain," he said thickly. "As long as your heart beats and you have an ounce of breath in you, they, too, still exist. That is what sustains us, knowing that we hold within us someone dear who may have passed on to the other side physically, yet spiritually remains still in the heart. Your parents will always be there to reach for so you still feel loved."

"That is such a beautiful way to think about it," Nicole said, marveling anew at this man's ability to make her feel better about herself and her life.

She had felt such emptiness when she thought of how her parents had died. Now this wonderful man had explained to her how that emptiness could be filled with love and precious memories.

"I am telling you what I was told when I lost someone precious to me when I was a child," Eagle Wolf said thickly. "It was a sister who died.

In age, she came between myself and my brother. My sister left this world when she was only seven winters of age. She strayed too far from the safety circle of our people and lost her footing at the edge of a bluff. The entire village searched and searched for her when it was discovered that she had wandered from the village, alone. It was I who looked down from that bluff and saw her lying there so quiet . . . so . . . dead . . . so broken."

"How horrible," Nicole gasped. "You were too young to experience such a terrible thing as that. I am so sorry, Eagle Wolf. So very sorry."

He smiled and placed his hand over his heart once again. "Remember? My sister is not gone," he said softly. "She is here. I can feel her. I can see her. She is always with me, to make my day brighter. When I lay so ill with fever, she was there stroking my brow with a soft, cool cloth. I was too weak to awaken and thank her."

Nicole's eyes widened, for he had just described how she had sat there while he was unconscious with the worst of his fever. She herself had stroked his brow with the cool water she had brought from the stream.

She saw now how he might have believed that his sister had done this, for Nicole knew there was a part of Eagle Wolf that wanted it to be his sister.

"You can bring your parents into your mind's eye however you wish to see them, and I know that you want to see them the way you remember them before the tragedy struck," Eagle Wolf said, nodding. "Is that not so?"

"Yes, it is," Nicole murmured.

An owl hooting from somewhere in the shadows interrupted their conversation, causing them both to look in that direction.

"Voices in the night that I am familiar with," Eagle Wolf said, laughing softly. "And I believe that voice is telling me it is time for us to go to our blankets. Tomorrow is not so far away."

He stood up and walked around the fire to Nicole. He bent down, gathered a blanket into his arms, and then held it out for her.

"Again you will sleep on this side of the fire and I, the other," he said solemnly as their eyes met and held.

Nicole felt so much for him at this moment, it was hard not to fling herself into his arms and thank him over and over again for his kindness. He had made her feel so much better about everything.

He had such a mystical way of talking and thinking.

She longed to stay so that she could be with him forever.

When she gazed deep into his eyes, and saw emotion that matched her own feelings for him, she found it hard to believe that she would leave him tonight and surely never see him again, unless . . .

Unless he wanted her as badly as she wanted him, and came searching for her.

If he did find her, would he feel comfortable enough to take her to his home with him? Would he ignore how his people might feel about her?

She blinked her eyes in order to stop herself from thinking these things.

She smiled and accepted the blanket. Then she watched as he went and stretched out on his own.

Nicole spread her blanket and lay down upon it, fighting her feelings as each moment passed. Soon she would tiptoe into the darkness and perhaps never see him again.

She hated to think that she might never see his beautiful eyes and smile again, or feel that fleeting touch that seemed oh, so magical and sweet.

She ached for his arms!

She ached for his kiss!

She ached with all of her heart at what she must do.

As Eagle Wolf lay there, he wrestled with his own feelings. He knew how alone Nicole was in the world now, yet he also knew how much his people hated the white eyes.

He must trust that she would find her way to a white community. That was the only way it could be.

But he knew that he would always carry a sense of no longer being whole. This woman completed him.

Without her, life would be so lonely, so empty.

Yet he saw no other course except to tell her good-bye on the morrow.

It would be sad, but necessary.

Finally he fell asleep, only to have fitful dreams of watching Nicole ride away, his arms outstretched as he begged her not to go.

It seemed only a matter of moments since he had gone to sleep beneath the crescent moon, yet there it was dawn already, the birds overhead awakening him.

Believing he would find Nicole on the other side of the campfire, Eagle Wolf leaned up on an elbow to say good morning to her.

When he saw that Nicole was not there, he sat up quickly and looked toward where her horse had been tethered. It was gone, too. His heart sank, for he knew now that she had left while he slept.

He realized that she, too, would have found it hard to look into his eyes to say good-bye. He knew that she loved him as deeply as he loved her.

He was not certain how love could come so quickly and completely, but it had. Yet now that she was gone, he must leave, too, and return to his life . . . without her.

Dispirited, he rose from his blanket and prepared his horse for leaving.

Although he ached to hold Nicole and keep and protect her, *ka-bike-hozhoni-bi*, happy evermore, he mounted his horse and rode away in the direction of his home.

Yet he could not stop thinking about Nicole and where she might be, and whether or not she would remain safe.

It was hard not to wheel his horse around and go after her.

Suddenly he saw the wolf that he had saved from its terrible injuries. It was elusive, but seemed to always be near, somehow, staring at him with its mystical, yellow eyes.

And then, as always before, it suddenly ran away into the darkness of the trees.

Eagle Wolf's eyes searched for the wolf a moment longer, and then he set his full attention on returning home.

Today he had lost two beings that he had grown to love.

The woman.

And the wolf.

He hoped someday he would see them both again.

Chapter Thirteen

As the morning brought its sweetness to the land, with birds singing and the sky so blue and peaceful, Sam Partain sat in his saddle. His gang surrounded him as he paused in the shadowy depths of a forest of birch trees.

From this vantage point, Sam could see a small settlement in the distance.

He knew about it. This was a settlement of Mormons. He had never been there before, but he had heard about it.

He had thought long and hard about where Nicole might go when she found Tyler City burned out. He had concluded that she would be too afraid to go to the mountain to hide, for she had to know that the Navaho were entrenched there in their stronghold.

What woman wasn't afraid of Indians?

And since the nearest fort was so far away, Sam had surmised that she would surely go to the closest place to find sanctuary.

Yep, he might even now be looking at that very place.

He cackled to himself as he thought about the men who lived in Mormon towns. Did they not make it a practice to take more than one wife?

Now, if given the opportunity, who wouldn't want Nicole as one of those wives? He had admired her beauty in St. Louis. She was petite and beautiful, with fiery red hair that hung down to her waist.

Sam laughed throatily as he recalled how clear she had made it that she had no interest in good ol' boy Sam Partain. Well, soon she'd have no choice about associating with him.

"Do you think she's there?" A voice broke through Sam's thoughts.

He turned and gazed at his right-hand man, Ace Koontz. "I'd bet my bottom dollar on it," Sam said, snickering.

He stroked his scraggly golden beard as he again looked at the town called Hope. "Yep," he said thickly. "She just might have gone to those Mormons for help. Well, there's no time like the present for this ol' boy to find out."

"Want us to go with you?" Ace asked, tilting his head slightly sideways as he was wont to do.

His black hair hung to his waist, and his skin was sun bronzed. At a distance, he might be mistaken for an Indian. But up close, his sea blue eyes showed that he was a white man.

"Naw, not yet, anyhow," Sam said, tightening his hold on his reins. "I'll go in, sololike, and ask whether that pretty thing is there or not."

"How are you going to get them to give you answers, you bein' a stranger and all?" Ace asked as Sam turned to look into his eyes once again. "If'n she saw the massacre, might'nt she have warned those people not to trust anyone who comes to ask 'bout her?"

"I know what I'm doin', so shut yore mouth, Ace, do you hear?" Sam said. He almost reached out to slap Ace, but stopped short of doing it. He had more things on his mind besides reminding one of his men that he was the boss.

"Sorry, boss," Ace said, tucking his head, so that his pointed chin almost touched his chest.

"I'll be leavin' you now, boys," Sam said. "Sit tight. I shouldn't be long. If she's there with the Mormons, hiding out, God be with them, for I won't bat an eye over killin' 'em all in order to get that pretty thing all to myself."

He laughed throatily as he broke away from his men and rode out into the clearing. He galloped off, leaving his gang hidden among the shadows of yellow-leafed birch trees.

He knew it was best that he go alone. A lone rider wouldn't seem suspicious to the townsfolk.

Anyway, he hoped not.

If Nicole was there, hiding, would they be able to keep this truth from Sam?

Only time would tell, and he would soon have his answers, because a man was riding toward him even now, a rifle in his right hand, his horse's reins in the other.

The man's face had a suspicious look as he gave Sam the quick once-over, stopping his horse a few feet from him.

"You are riding toward Hope," the man said guardedly as he glared at Sam. He sat stiffly in the saddle in his black suit, and his face displayed a very neatly shaped red beard.

"Nice to make your acquaintance," the man then said, yet did not offer a handshake.

"My name's Aaron," he went on. "Aaron Smith. What's yours, and do you have a reason to be headed in the direction of Hope?"

Sam didn't have a chance to answer before another black-suited man rode up and positioned himself beside Aaron.

"What's he got to say about being headed toward Hope like he has business there?" the second man asked as he glanced over at Aaron, and then back at Sam.

"He hasn't said, Jeremiah," Aaron replied.

"Now it's your turn to talk," Jeremiah said smoothly as he gazed intently at Sam. "Where you headed? Where you coming from?"

Jeremiah looked past Sam, searching for the possibility of other riders who might be this man's traveling companions.

"Yep, I was headed for your fine town, and for a reason," Sam said tightly. He looked past both men at the women, men, and children who had congregated at the edge of town. They were anxiously watching what was happening.

"What is that reason?" Jeremiah prodded.

"I'm looking for a woman who was supposed to arrive in Tyler City to join her ma and pa," Sam said, trying to look innocent. "You see, I'm a friend of her pa's. I was gone when the tragedy struck. If you don't know 'bout it, let me explain. Someone came while I was away from town and killed off everyone. I am the lone survivor. Well, I was a close friend to Walter Tyler and his wife, and I knew that Nicole was supposed to arrive there any day. I did not find her among the dead. I thought she might have come to you for help and you might've offered to take her in."

Sam frowned at Jeremiah. "Did it happen that way?" he asked thickly. "Did my friend's daughter show up here, frightened to death, and all?"

Jeremiah was a very astute man and knew a liar when he saw one. He could tell by the way a person's eyes moved as he told the lie.

This man's eyes had shifted nervously from Jeremiah over to Aaron and back to Jeremiah. He was nervous about what he was saying, too nervous for it to be the truth.

And there was a hint of evil in his gray eyes.

Then it occurred to Jeremiah that this man might be one of those who'd killed everyone in Tyler City. And if this was one of those murdering men, perhaps the others were hiding somewhere close and waiting for him to come to them with answers.

Jeremiah knew that the lives of all of the people

of Hope might depend on him being able to keep calm in the face of danger. He had to say all of the right things to make this man ride away, and leave him and the others in peace.

"I don't know of anyone named Nicole," he said tightly, knowing that sometimes lies were necessary. This was one of those times. "But I hope you find her. It is terrible that so many people died in such a way. It would be sad if this girl is lost now, too."

"And so you haven't seen her, or heard of her?" Sam persisted. Jeremiah shook his head.

"Well, then, gents, I'll be on my way," Sam said. He gave both men a half salute. "Thanks for your time and trouble."

"Don't mention it," Jeremiah said, breathing more easily now that the stranger had wheeled his horse around and headed back in the direction whence he had come.

Aaron wiped beads of sweat from his brow, and Jeremiah did the same. "That was a close one," he said, his voice crackling with the fear that still had him in its grip.

"Way, way too close," Jeremiah agreed. He turned back toward Hope, and set out with Aaron riding beside him. "Aaron, that man was lying through his teeth. We must post more sentries around our town. We can't take chances."

He looked slowly over his shoulder, then gasped and grew pale when he saw Sam Partain reach a thick grouping of birch trees. Several men on horses came out of the shadows to join him.

Jeremiah scarcely breathed as he waited to see in which direction those men would ride.

When the men headed away from Hope, Jeremiah sighed with relief. Then he put his heels to the flanks of his horse and rode more hurriedly toward the town, Aaron following him.

After arriving in the town, and explaining to everyone the possible danger, Jeremiah had one more thing to say to them. "Be wary of this man who came today. He walks in sheep's clothing, but is in truth a man of Satan!" he shouted, as the men began scattering in many directions, their hands now clasped tight on their rifles.

Wanting to see about his own family before going to take a guard post himself, Jeremiah went and gathered his wives and children around him and ushered them back to their house.

He bent on a knee as he held the children close while his wives looked on, their eyes filled with tears of fear.

"That man of Satan asked about that nice lady who rode the stagecoach with us," Jeremiah explained softly. "No one knows where she is, or if she is even still alive. I pray that those men don't find her. They do not have anything good planned for her—that is certain."

To himself he was thinking that he hoped Nicole was still alive and that he could find her someday. But not now. It was too dangerous to think about searching for her again.

He still wanted to have Nicole as his third wife. She could give him beautiful, strong sons, he was sure.

His two wives would not want him to take another wife, yet they knew better than to argue. His word was law in his household.

But . . . where could Nicole have gone? Would those men find her before Jeremiah felt it was safe enough to go and look for her again, himself?

He just could not get her out of his mind, or blood, no matter how hard he had tried. If she was still alive, he wanted her, and . . . he . . . would have her.

But only if that group of bloodthirsty men didn't find her first!

Chapter Fourteen

As Eagle Wolf entered his village, he felt a wonderful sense of homecoming. When everyone saw that it was he, they came running toward him.

He had always known the love his people felt for him, but the proof of it touched his heart. It was in everyone's eyes, their outstretched arms, their shouts of happiness. They were overjoyed at his return and that he had survived.

As he rode slowly onward, he saw that a new tepee had been built close by the spot where his home had sat before he had set fire to it.

He smiled a quiet thank-you to his people, then went onward. When he reached his newly erected tepee, his brother stepped suddenly from the lodge.

Eagle Wolf dismounted and stepped toward Spirit Wolf, to embrace him. But his brother walked past him without a greeting, without a smile, his head hanging low.

It ate into Eagle Wolf's heart to know from his brother's sulking attitude just how much he had hoped Eagle Wolf would not come back.

With Eagle Wolf's return came the end of Spirit Wolf's own temporary reign as chief. It was oh, so obvious that Spirit Wolf had wanted to remain his people's chief forever.

He had surely even prayed that Eagle Wolf would not return.

Their people now also witnessed the behavior of one brother toward the other. Some gasped in horror as they watched Spirit Wolf disappear into his own lodge without speaking a single word to his brother.

Wanting to break the awkward silence, Eagle Wolf handed his reins to a young brave, who took his steed away. Eagle Wolf faced his people, who stood there with love for him in their eyes and smiles.

"My people, it is good to be among you again," Eagle Wolf said, taking the hand of a small child, a young boy of five winters who gazed lovingly up at him. "The disease that made me so ill, and killed my wife, was not smallpox, but instead a white man's disease called measles. I survived. I am well. I will now resume my duties as your chief."

"What is this thing called measles?" one of his warriors asked as he stepped closer to Eagle Wolf. His eyes moved slowly over his chief, taking in the fading red spots on his body. "How do you know of it?"

"A woman found me when I was feverish and stopped to care for me," Eagle Wolf said, purposely not telling them that this woman was white, or that she had found her way inside his heart. "She explained to me that the red spots were measles, not smallpox."

"What woman?" another warrior asked. "Where is she now?"

Although it was not his habit to ignore questions asked him by his people, Eagle Wolf did not want to talk about Nicole Tyler. He did not want to reveal to his people that she was white.

"Is it not enough that I am with you again, and that I am well?" Eagle Wolf asked.

There was a strange sort of silence brought on by his obvious reluctance to speak any more of this mysterious woman. To break the awkward moment, he turned and gazed at the large, new tepee.

"This is a very fine lodge," he said, lifting the entrance flap and looking around inside before entering.

What he saw made his eyes widen. He had not expected to see any belongings in the lodge since everything he had owned had been burned.

But what he saw had nothing to do with him at all. Although there were only a few items, he recognized them as the possessions of his brother and his wife.

He turned and looked questioningly at the warrior closest to his side.

"Your brother and wife were moving their belongings today into the tepee that was built for you, my chief," Three Bears said uncomfortably.

"No one questioned him because he was at that time acting chief."

Three Bears looked over at the tepee where Spirit Wolf had gone, and then at Eagle Wolf again. "His lodge still stands, yet it would have not been his by evening. By then all of his belongings would have been in the tepee that was built for your return."

"He did not expect my recovery," Eagle Wolf said thickly.

"Seems not," Three Bears said. "I believe he prayed that you would not return. He is a brother who should no longer be called a brother. He never should have had the title of chief, not even for a short while. Chiefs are chosen for wisdom and high character, and Spirit Wolf has neither."

Eagle Wolf listened to those words with an aching heart. He loved his younger brother, but was not proud of him.

He nodded at Three Bears, to let him know that he had heard him and respected his feelings, but Eagle Wolf needed time alone now, for he had much to think about.

After stepping into his new lodge, he again looked slowly around at his brother's belongings. He knew that there was only one thing to do. He began by taking one item and then another and tossing them outside on the ground, as his people watched, silent.

As each thing was thrown from his lodge, Eagle Wolf became angrier and angrier at Spirit

Wolf. His brother had proved his disloyalty and lack of love.

Eagle Wolf was disappointed, but glad that he knew of his brother's betrayal. No longer would he be made a fool of by a brother who felt nothing but jealousy toward him.

When everything had finally been cleared from his lodge, Eagle Wolf went inside, alone.

He was dispirited as he sat on a mat before the freshly made fire. The firelight now shone brightly on a face that revealed his shock over the truth of his brother's feelings toward him. He felt a disappointment in Spirit Wolf that would surely stay with Eagle Wolf until death.

Suddenly his thoughts were interrupted. One by one, his people came to him, speaking his name outside his lodge.

And when he went and held the entrance flap aside, he saw each one's arms heavy-laden with gifts for him.

There were clothes, blankets, food, and even a newly carved bow, as well as a quiver of arrows. One little girl handed him her doll made from corn husks, a small blanket wrapped around it.

And after those gifts from the heart were all taken into his lodge and put into place, more food arrived, this time stacked high on platters.

There was his favorite . . . mutton stew, with corn cooked in it, and so many other delicious things made by the women of his village.

Before settling down to eat, Eagle Wolf stepped

from his lodge where his people were gathered. They had gone to great lengths to prove that they still were loyal to him, and loved him.

He quickly noticed that his brother's belongings were gone from the spot where Eagle Wolf had tossed them.

He supposed his brother had hurriedly come and gotten them while Eagle Wolf was inside his own lodge.

"How can I thank you all enough for your love and loyalty to me?" Eagle Wolf asked. He looked slowly around the crowd. He was touched deeply by the love his people had shown him. He would always remember this moment.

"No thanks are needed," Three Bears said, giving Eagle Wolf one of his most vivid smiles. "Your return to us is all we could ever want."

"I will remember today and what you have done for me, always," Eagle Wolf said, getting a quick glimpse of his brother as he momentarily drew his entrance flap aside in order to look at Eagle Wolf, and then disappeared again in his lodge.

Eagle Wolf smiled at his people, then turned and went back inside his tepee. He sat down and began eating the delicious food that had been prepared for his homecoming.

As he ate beside the fire, his legs crossed at his ankles, he could not help thinking about Nicole and worrying about her.

He could not help wondering if she had found a safe haven.

Or was she still wandering, alone, lost and afraid?

He made himself push her from his mind. She was not his concern.

He was home with his people, where he belonged. All of his attention should be on them and on them alone!

Chapter Fifteen

Jeremiah was riding with several men who had volunteered to join him as he continued to search for Nicole Tyler. Jeremiah's eyes looked in all directions as he rode onward, while the five men with him did the same.

He was not hunting for Nicole out of the goodness of his heart, but because he was determined to have her as his third wife. No, there would be no convincing him otherwise.

If he went to the trouble of finding her and taking her to safety, she would owe him, and the debt would be paid by her speaking vows with him.

But he wouldn't hurry her to the altar. If he did find her, he would have to take it slow convincing her to be his wife.

He had to remember that she was not of the Mormon faith. She would not believe in the tenet of a man taking more than one wife.

But Jeremiah would make certain that she learned of his faith, understood and accepted it. And then he would tell her his plan; that he wanted her to be his third wife.

He knew that he might be placing himself and the men who rode with him in danger by looking for Nicole. He knew that there were others looking for her, too, who would probably not think twice about shooting him and his friends on sight.

Jeremiah did feel guilty for asking his friends to join him on this dangerous venture, but once he'd set his mind on rescuing Nicole, nothing would make him turn back. He was bound and determined to find her and to have her.

Ah, but he would treat her so grandly, even though by doing so, he would make his other two wives very jealous. But that didn't matter to him.

He was the voice of their family. His wives would have no choice but to accept another wife among them. And eventually the children that Nicole would bring into their lives, as well.

He envisioned this pretty thing with the fiery red hair smiling at him, actually loving him, and wanting him as badly as he wanted her.

Yes, it would happen. She would stay with him willingly after she got to know him better and realized that he was a man she could learn to love.

"Let's ride hard, gents," Jeremiah said as he snapped his reins and sank his heels into the flanks of his mount. "I hope to find Nicole before the sun starts sinking in the west."

"I doubt that we will," Jacob said, turning a frown toward him. "Just think of it, Jeremiah. What are the chances of finding her?"

"No matter what, we won't give up until we see the sun sinking in the sky," Jeremiah said. "Only then will we think of heading back toward home. I understand your feelings. We have our children and wives to consider."

"I'm glad to hear you say that," Jacob replied tightly. "For a while there I thought this woman was all that you were thinking about, and you know that no woman is worth risking our lives."

"Yet you are here with me," Jeremiah noted. "Thank you, Jacob, for being such a good friend. One day I'll repay you in kind."

"No need," Jacob said. "No need at all. I'm just glad you realize that when dusk falls, we have to head back for home. If we live long enough," he added under his breath.

"What's that you say?" Jeremiah asked, lifting his eyebrows.

"You heard me," Jacob grumbled. "You heard me."

Chapter Sixteen

The mountain paths were so confusing to Nicole, she felt as though she had been riding in circles all day. She wondered if she had gotten anywhere.

Only a few moments ago she had finally reached the base of the mountain. She just hoped that she had come down on the opposite side from where Tyler City lay in ashes. She hoped that she was far enough away that Sam Partain and his gang would not be able to find her.

She had a campfire going, so that when darkness fell all around her, she would not have to fear animals coming up on her in the dark. The flames would frighten wild beasts sniffing around in the dark.

But they might attract other animals to her . . . two-legged ones.

She sat on her blanket beside the fire, her rifle resting on her lap. She had gathered berries for her supper, but she was not looking forward to eating them. She had eaten so many these past days just to have something in her stomach.

She closed her eyes and thought of Eagle Wolf and how wonderful it would be to still be with him.

With her belly growling from hunger, she thought about the rabbit that he had cooked over the campfire. She had never eaten anything so delicious.

Thinking of Eagle Wolf caused a strange sort of ache in Nicole's heart, worse even than the ache in her belly from hunger.

Although they had been together for such a short time, it was long enough for him to speak to her heart in every way possible.

She looked toward the shadows of the aspen trees behind her, at the path that worked its way through them. If she were to follow that path, would she eventually find the Navaho stronghold?

Oh, how she missed Eagle Wolf.

She wondered how he had felt when he had awakened and found her gone. Had he attempted to find her? Or had he gone on to his stronghold, feeling better off without her, a white woman?

Emptying her skirt pocket of the berries, laying them on the blanket before her, she eyed them, shivering at the thought of eating even one more.

She wasn't sure how many more days she could survive without more substantial food. She needed strength to travel onward and find someone who would take mercy upon her and invite her into their dwelling.

Oh, but just to have one night in a cabin, with a family and a delicious home-cooked meal!

It would be like a dream. Strange, how only a few weeks ago, she had never thought to be day-dreaming about such things.

Her world had been perfect. Her parents had been alive, and she was about to embark on her new teaching career, something she had wanted since she'd been a student herself.

She had noticed how those children who seemed not to care about learning suddenly took interest. It was the teacher's encouragement that caused the change in their attitude.

She had wanted to be one of those special teachers, and maybe she would still be able to reach that goal.

But first, she had to stay alive. She had to get back to civilization.

She would have to put the deaths of her parents behind her. She would even have to learn how to forget Eagle Wolf, even though she knew he had etched a place inside her heart, like leaves fossilized into stone.

She must do everything within her power to survive this horrible ordeal, and that meant eating berries when there was nothing else to eat.

She reached for a berry and thrust it into her mouth. She almost choked on the juice as she heard the sound of horses approaching from somewhere to her right side.

She quickly swallowed, grabbed her rifle, then stood up and aimed it at the hidden riders.

It was so dark now. It was almost impossible to see beyond the campfire.

She wanted to cry out and ask who was there, yet her voice seemed stuck in her throat where the sweet berry taste lingered.

But it wasn't the taste of berries that had stolen her ability to speak. It was fear.

She was afraid that at any moment she would see Sam Partain.

She was tempted to fire blindly at those who were approaching. Oh, surely it was Sam Partain and his murdering scoundrel friends. Her campfire must have drawn them right to her.

They would surely rape her before they killed her. Would he and his men use her as their "toy" for days upon end, before tiring of her and murdering her?

Her legs almost buckled beneath her with relief when she was finally able to see the lead rider. It was Jeremiah Schrock, mounted upon a fine horse, with several other bearded men following his lead.

"Jeremiah!" Nicole cried, quickly lowering her rifle to her side. "Oh, Lordy be, Jeremiah! I was so afraid it was . . ."

"I'm sorry if we frightened you," Jeremiah said, close enough now to dismount.

The others stopped and dismounted, too, one

of them taking Jeremiah's reins so that he would be free to go to Nicole.

That was when Nicole broke down.

She dropped her rifle as tears blinded her. She had truly thought that she was living the last moments of her life.

The moment was ripe. Jeremiah saw this as the perfect opportunity to reach out for Nicole and hold her.

He could sense her distress over what she had suffered these past days. And wanting her so badly, he could not pass up this opportunity to try to ease some of Nicole's pain.

He reached for Nicole and drew her into his warm embrace.

He enjoyed the way she clung to him as her body was racked with sobs.

He smiled over his shoulder at Jacob. He was pleased that the others were witness to this woman accepting Jeremiah as a true, trusted friend, and perhaps . . . even more than that.

Nicole was suddenly aware of where she was, in whose arms. She had grown to dislike this man while traveling on the stagecoach with him.

She suddenly remembered how he had looked at her then, with lust in his eyes. She had felt it in the way he had just held her. His embrace had been possessive, not tender.

She stepped away from him and smiled awkwardly as she wiped the final tears from her eyes.

"I'm sorry," she murmured. "For a moment there I forgot myself. I was so afraid when I heard the horses, that it would be men out to harm me."

She swallowed hard, looked deeply into Jeremiah's eyes, then, almost timidly, asked, "I don't have a reason to be afraid, do I?"

She glanced around her, at the other men, who were now standing beside their horses, their eyes directly on her.

"How can you ask such a thing?" Jeremiah said, his eyes widening. "Have I ever given you reason to be afraid of me? Nicole, a man came to Hope, inquiring about you. I got the sense that he was up to no good and decided it was best that I find you first."

"What was his name?" Nicole blurted out. "By chance, was he . . . an . . . Indian?"

"No, he wasn't an Indian." Jeremiah looked at her through squinting eyes, wondering why she would ask about an Indian.

Had one accosted her on the trail?

Nicole sighed heavily, cold fear gripping her at the thought of who this man surely was.

Sam Partain!

He had been close to finding her, for she was sure that Jeremiah and his men had not come far to find her.

"Did he have long, dirty blond hair?" Nicole blurted out, afraid to hear the answer.

"Yes, and eyes that made a chill ride my spine. His eyes reflected the devil in them," Jeremiah said, visibly shuddering. "Do you know of him? Do you know his name?"

"Yes, I believe Sam Partain paid you a visit," Nicole said grimly. Her eyes widened. "But if he was alone, perhaps I am wrong. This gutless man rides with a group of murdering, heartless outlaws."

"He came to Hope alone, pretending to be someone of decent breeding, and asked about you. When I told him, or should I say convinced him, that you were not there, he rode off," Jeremiah said tightly. "I watched him for a while longer and then I saw several men on horseback come from the shadows of the forest and join him. They rode off together."

"Then that was Sam Partain for certain," Nicole said, so glad that tonight she had been discovered by a group of Mormon men, not murdering outlaws.

"How do you know this man?" Jeremiah prodded.

"Sam Partain and his gang are responsible for the deaths of my parents and everyone else who joined my father in his new town of Tyler City," Nicole said, tears rushing to her eyes again at the thought of her parents lying there, hand in hand, bullet holes in their brows.

"Why would he kill everyone so heartlessly?" Jeremiah asked. "I witnessed the devastation this man and his followers left behind."

"You did?" Nicole asked, her eyes wide.

"Word was brought to me about what had

happened in Tyler City," Jeremiah answered. "I immediately thought of you since I knew that was your destination. Several of my friends and I rode there to see if, by chance, you had survived. I did not see you anywhere, so I hoped that you had somehow escaped the massacre. Before we left, we took the time to bury those who had died."

"You . . . buried . . . them?" Nicole asked, stunned by the kindness of these men. She regretted her ugly thoughts about Jeremiah. "You . . . actually buried my parents?

"Thank you," she added, humbly lowering her eyes.

"It was my duty to bury them," Jeremiah said thickly.

Jeremiah's eyebrows lifted. "How have you survived since?" he asked softly. "You are all alone . . ."

She didn't want to tell him about Eagle Wolf. She knew that it was best not to draw any undue attention his way.

He was a man who lived in hiding, and did so for a reason. He would not want anyone to have cause to seek him out.

She had fled so that he would be safe and could return to his people.

"I'm not sure, myself, how I've done it," Nicole said, her voice breaking. She lowered her eyes again. "I wasn't certain how much longer I could go on."

"Well, young lady, that is no longer a problem you have to think about," Jeremiah said, smiling broadly as Nicole looked quickly up at him. "I have come to offer you shelter, safety, and a place to use your teaching skills. Come with me and my friends and you will have a home, and a teaching position. You can teach our Mormon children. Soon we were going to look for a teacher. Seems our prayers have been answered by your coming into our lives. Will you join us in Hope, Nicole?"

Nicole could not shake off the feeling of mistrust she'd had while riding with Jeremiah in the stagecoach. But learning that he had buried the dead in Tyler City caused her to see this man in a different light.

And she was so happy that she would not have to spend another minute alone in the wilderness, hiding from the madmen who were searching for her.

She smiled and thrust out a hand toward Jeremiah for a handshake. Her father had taught her that even though she was a lady, a firm handshake showed she was a woman of strength.

"It's a deal," she said, smiling broadly at Jeremiah, wanting to laugh when she saw how stunned he was at her outthrust hand.

"I'd love to be your town's schoolmarm," she quickly added. "Let's shake on it."

Jeremiah smiled crookedly, not knowing

whether or not to be amused at this strange behavior.

He had to remember that this woman was different in many ways. She was better educated than most of the men of Hope, and had far more education than the women, who for the most part, had none at all.

Yes, he had himself a special woman in Nicole. She would make life a mite interesting, now, wouldn't she?

He reached out and gripped Nicole's hand. "A deal," he said, glancing over his shoulder at the men, who were gawking at what was transpiring between him and the beautiful lady.

He held her hand a moment longer, then helped her gather up her things as Jacob threw handfuls of dirt on the fire.

Jeremiah walked Nicole to her horse and helped her into the saddle, then mounted his own steed.

Soon they were headed back in the direction of Hope and Nicole had a chance to consider this latest turn of events.

She had been rescued just as she had hoped. She only wished that Eagle Wolf hadn't accepted her having left him.

She couldn't help being disappointed that he hadn't came for her after seeing that she had left the campsite. Had he found her, she would have gone with him to his stronghold in an instant, for she knew that she truly loved him.

Feeling foolish to be thinking about Eagle Wolf, and what might have been, Nicole concentrated on her future.

Thanks to Jeremiah, she now had a future, even if it would be without the man she loved.

Chapter Seventeen

As the early morning sun swept down through the smoke hole above Eagle Wolf, he tossed fitfully in his blankets, then awakened and sat up quickly.

It was a dream that had awakened him with such a start. Even now there were pearls of sweat on his brow as he thought of it and how real it had seemed.

This dream had been like no other he had ever had. He had dreamed of a woman he could not forget.

Nicole.

In his dream he had seen her in danger. Two men had been on each side of her, pulling her first one way, and then another.

In the dream she had fainted from fear, but before she had fallen to the ground, she had called out Eagle Wolf's name.

He could hear her voice now, as though she were there, her eyes pleading with him, her arms outstretched toward him as she begged him to help her.

He knew that when someone had such a dream, one that seemed so real, it meant something.

It did not take him long to interpret this dream.

He believed he was being beckoned by Nicole to come and find her and bring her back with him to his village. There she would be safe, *ka-bike-hozhoni-bi*, happy forevermore.

An ache deep inside told him now that he should never have allowed her to leave as she had. He should have gone to bring her back to him.

She was oh, so alone in the world . . . except for him.

Ho, dreams spoke true. Nicole was in trouble and needed him. He must go and find her.

He hurriedly pulled on his fringed buckskin breeches and shirt and slid his feet into his moccasins.

He combed his fingers through his thick black hair to rid it of tangles. He quickly slipped on a beaded headband, secured his sheathed knife at his right side, then grabbed his rifle. Before he left his tepee, he recalled the dream once again, to see if something about it that he had not remembered earlier might come to him to help him in his pursuit of this woman.

He clenched his eyes closed in an attempt to remember identifying characteristics of the men in his dream who were a threat to Nicole. He had not seen their faces, just their clothes.

One wore all black, such as he had seen Mormon men wear.

The other man had long, filthy golden hair that fell down his back, and he wore crude, dirty clothes.

The dream had surely meant that those two men were fighting over Nicole. If the dream were true, then would he find her soon enough to rescue her?

He must!

Or he would always regret having allowed himself to fall asleep beside the fire that night. How could he have missed realizing her plan when she had said good night to him so sadly? Surely she had said those words knowing that when he awakened in the morning, she would be gone.

Ho, he must find her. And when he did, he would take her under his wing and protect her, not only for now, but forever.

With determination etched on his sculpted face, and his jaw tight, Eagle Wolf strode from his lodge and went to stand in the center of his stronghold.

In a loud, stern voice, he awakened everyone, calling his warriors to him.

"My warriors, I should apologize for pulling you from your beds in such a way, but I will not," Eagle Wolf began. "I have asked you to come to me this early morning because there is something that must be done and I need ten of you to go with me today. I shall point those ten out and the rest can return to your lodges and families. As we ride, I will explain to you why we are leaving our homes, even without our early morning meal. Ready yourselves. I will wait for you at my corral."

He chose his men, and then went to his corral and readied his white stallion, mounted it, and waited for all of the ten warriors to come to him on their own steeds.

And when they did arrive, the group rode from the stronghold together. Only when they were far from the tepees and riding down the pass did Eagle Wolf raise a fist in the air, a silent command for them to stop.

He wheeled his horse around and faced his warriors. "There is a woman..." he began, watching their eyes and their expressions as he explained what he expected of them today.

He could tell by their faces that some did not agree with their chief's plan, while the others showed their support. They loved their chief and would be there for him, always, no matter what he might ask of them. If he wanted to find this woman, even a woman whose skin was white, so be it.

"It might take more than one day—are you prepared to ride with me until we find the woman?" Eagle Wolf asked, again looking slowly from man to man. "This is the chance for you to return to your families should you wish to. If not,

I expect you to follow my direction until we finally have the woman safely with us."

No one turned back.

Eagle Wolf smiled warmly at each of them, then turned his horse back down the mountain.

He could not get the dream from his mind. If the men in his dream were real and had taken Nicole by force, would Eagle Wolf ever find her? Would he be able to turn back without her and again forget her?

He gazed heavenward and spoke a silent prayer to his Great Spirit. He prayed that what he was doing was right and that he would soon be riding into his village with the flame-haired woman at his side.

Back at the stronghold, Eagle Wolf's brother, Spirit Wolf, smiled to himself as he sat beside his lodge fire, thinking about his brother having left the safety of the stronghold again.

No matter what had taken Eagle Wolf away again, this time he would surely not return. Eagle Wolf was taking too many chances, too often.

Spirit Wolf's smile faded as he wondered what had taken his brother away again. What could be out there, beckoning him from his home again?

Spirit Wolf did not really care. All he knew was that if his brother did not return home, Spirit Wolf would be appointed chief by his people again, and this time he would remain so, forever!

He did not care about the safety of a brother who had been favored above Spirit Wolf all of Spirit Wolf's life.

What was fair about that?

But fairness would soon show its face to his people, by demonstrating that Spirit Wolf was meant to be their chief, not Eagle Wolf.

Chapter Eighteen

Today was Nicole's very first as a teacher and she could not help being apprehensive. Although she had studied hard and knew all that she needed to know to be a good teacher, she was still anxious.

She had been given no reason to feel uncomfortable with her new situation. The people of Hope had been nothing but kind to her since her arrival there.

They had given her a house all to herself, fully furnished. It was small, but large enough for her since she had brought nothing into this new world except her one travel bag of clothing, and now a horse that she called her own.

She looked around the one-room schoolhouse where she would soon greet the children on her first day as a teacher. She walked slowly around the room, absently touching one desk and then another. She glanced at her own desk, which sat facing these. She had already printed her name in big letters on the chalkboard.

She walked slowly to the door, then stood aside when the children began coming into the room. She recognized the four little girls who had been on the stagecoach with her. They were the daughters of the very man who'd come to her rescue and brought her back to his settlement.

She would be forever grateful for his kindness. She only hoped that he hadn't had ulterior motives for going to so much trouble.

Earlier, when she had first met these girls, she had not been told their names. During the family's conversations in the stagecoach, she had discovered two of their names, but now could not even remember them.

She smiled at all four of the pretty little girls now as they stepped out of the way of the other children who were hurrying into the building.

Jeremiah's daughters' eyes were wide and their smiles were broad as they stood beside Nicole, each looking up at her with what seemed to be an expression of adoration. She could only guess that these pretty things were as anxious to have a teacher as she was to be one.

"It's so good to see you children again," Nicole said, smiling from one to the other. "I am embarrassed to say that I do not remember your names," she murmured.

"Mine is Hannah," the tiniest of the four spoke up, her dark eyes twinkling as she continued smiling at Nicole.

"Mine is Jane," one of the others said, smiling just as broadly and sweetly.

The other two children added their names quickly.

"Mine is Tara."

"Mine is Kathryn."

"Such pretty names for such pretty and sweet girls," Nicole murmured. "I am so grateful to your father for having brought me to Hope. I'm especially grateful for being given the chance to be your teacher. I have always longed to be a teacher. I cannot think of anyone I would enjoy teaching more than I will you."

"We're glad you are here, too," Hannah blurted out. She had a strange timid look as she lowered her eyes for a moment, then raised them again so she could look directly into Nicole's eyes. "My daddy is glad you are here, but Mama is not as pleased."

Nicole was not at all surprised to hear that, for she knew that the two women on the stagecoach had not been happy at her presence. They had completely ignored her.

Then she was stunned speechless as Hannah continued talking. "Mama said my father is going to marry you."

"Your father told your mother that he . . . that he . . . is going to take me as his third wife?" Nicole stammered.

"Yes, I heard Daddy telling Mama and my other mama that after you are here for a while and get to know everyone better, he will be asking you for your hand in marriage," Jane put in.

Hannah stepped closer to Nicole. "Will you please give us a brother?" she asked oh, so innocently.

"A brother?" Nicole repeated, paling at the thought of exactly where this conversation would take her.

She must leave this small and peaceful town of Hope as soon as she could.

That would take a lot of sneaking on her part, but she would never allow him the satisfaction of having her as his third wife.

Never!

"Daddy said he was going to give you time to get settled among our people and then he will tell you his plans," Tara piped in, her straight perfect teeth shining white in the sunlight coming through the schoolhouse door.

"I hope that won't be long," Jane blurted. "We want a brother real bad. Really, really bad."

"I'm sure you do," Nicole said tightly.

"Most of the other girls have brothers," Kathryn said. "We want one, too."

"I hope Daddy doesn't wait too long to stand up beside you," Jane then said. She nudged Kathryn in the ribs. "I think we'd better go and sit down. Everyone else has."

"Yes, let's," Kathryn said anxiously. "It will be such fun, Jane. We will finally learn our numbers!"

Nicole was stunned by what she had discovered. She was so angry, and felt so terribly betrayed, she could not stop trembling.

Nicole turned and looked across the town square at the house where Jeremiah's two wives stood on the porch. Her insides tightened when she saw how their arms were crossed as their eyes locked on Nicole.

Nicole felt an icy shiver ride her spine at the resentment she saw in the women's attitude. She thought that if she could read those two women's thoughts, she would learn that they would do anything to rid themselves of this woman they hated with a passion.

Her heart pounding, suddenly feeling this new threat with every beat of her heart, Nicole turned quickly, placing her back to the women.

She looked at all of the children, who now dutifully sat at their desks, waiting for their new teacher to begin teaching.

How could she carry on as if everything were normal? With all that she knew now, how could she behave as though nothing had happened?

One thing was certain. Her time in this settlement would be very short-lived.

She would never become anyone's third wife. She most certainly did not want to bear Jeremiah the son he was looking forward to.

Her thoughts went to Eagle Wolf.

Oh, how happy she would be to become *his* wife.

But she must forget him and think about this situation at hand.

Although she felt safe and protected at this settlement, Nicole knew she must leave Hope, and as soon as possible.

She didn't want to give Jeremiah one more minute of making plans for her to marry him.

Yet what about Sam Partain? With him out there somewhere, surely still looking for her, she might not survive another night riding alone. She had nowhere to go, and no one to truly care about what happened to her.

No matter how these thoughts frightened her, she knew that she must leave tonight when everyone else was asleep.

She went to a window and gazed toward the mountain. Up there, somewhere, was Eagle Wolf's stronghold.

Yes, that was where she would go. She would leave Hope tonight and find Eagle Wolf, for he was the only person who cared whether she lived or died.

A tiny voice drew her quickly back to the task at hand. Hannah had left her desk and was staring up at her.

Nicole bent low and gathered her in her arms. "Sweetie, go and take your seat," she murmured. "I plan to teach you and the other children some letters of the alphabet today."

"You look so sad suddenly," Hannah murmured.

She placed her tiny hands gently on Nicole's cheeks. "Why?"

"I'm not sad," Nicole said, trying to give the child a smile that looked sincere. She truly regretted having to take these children's dreams away.

She reached up, removed Hannah's hands from her cheeks and held them tenderly for a moment. "It's just that I want to be a good teacher," she murmured. "It's my first day, you know."

Hannah smiled. "You will be the best teacher in the world," she said, then went back to her desk and sat down.

Hannah smiled over her shoulder at Nicole, who still stood at the window. Nicole knew that this tiny child recognized Nicole's hesitance and was trying to reassure her that things would be all right.

Nicole returned the smile and felt sad about deceiving these children, especially these four sweet girls, for this was the one and only day she would be teaching them anything.

She hoped the town would find another teacher soon, as she could see the eagerness in these children's eyes to learn.

But Nicole most certainly could not be their teacher. Nor would she be the mother who would give the four sisters a brother.

She forced a smile on her face and hoped that she was hiding her stiffness as she went to the front of the room and stood at the chalkboard.

She picked up a piece of chalk and again printed her name in big letters. She pointed to each letter as she spoke it aloud to the children, then again told them her name.

"And now, children, which one of you wants to come to the chalkboard and learn how to print your name?" Nicole asked.

She smiled to herself, for she was not at all surprised when Hannah was the first to raise her hand.

"Me! Me!" Hannah said, eagerness in her dark brown eyes.

"Come, then, Hannah, and let the children see you print your name. Then you can choose who will be the next to place their name on the chalkboard beside yours," Nicole said.

Hannah printed her name, then turned with a broad smile and pointed to a boy her same age. "Adam," she said, not at all shy, as Nicole would have expected her to be at choosing a boy over the other girls.

Nicole could only smile at that, and love the child all the more for proving that she was an individual who could express her own wants and needs.

This child was someone special and Nicole hoped that Hannah would have the opportunity to follow her own dreams into the future, as Nicole had.

Nicole had thought and dreamed for so long of being a teacher. She had eagerly attended school and learned everything there was to learn in order to be the best teacher possible.

And now?

She would only teach for this one day and then must abandon her post. Now she doubted she would ever be able to teach. Surely it was just not meant to be.

She looked from the window again toward the mountain where her heart longed to be.

Eagle Wolf.

Oh, how she wanted to see him again. She prayed that when she went to that mountain again, she would find him and he would know that she had followed her heart.

He had shown such kindness and love while they were together. She knew that their destinies were intertwined.

She had to make certain they were intertwined forever.

Yes, she must find him!

And she would not let herself doubt the outcome of her search. When she was determined to accomplish something, there was no stopping her.

"Miss Tyler, is it my turn to go to the chalkboard and write my name?" Kathryn suddenly asked, breaking through Nicole's deep thoughts.

"Miss Tyler, can I?" Kathryn persisted. "Can I go now? Adam is finished writing his name. Can I? Can I have my turn?"

"Why, you most certainly can," Nicole said,

smiling at Kathryn while the child came up to the board and painstakingly wrote her name.

"Did I do it right?"

Nicole gazed at the clumsily printed letters, but nodded and smiled at Kathryn anyway. "It is very nicely done, Kathryn," she murmured. She turned to the children. "Let's give her applause, children. Doesn't she and the others deserve it since they did such a good job at the chalkboard?"

Big smiles came her way as the children began clapping their hands, making Nicole ache inside to know that on the morrow these children would have no reason to smile. They would come to the schoolhouse, but Nicole wouldn't be there to greet them.

Chapter Nineteen

Lingering longer beside the morning campfire than usual, Sam Partain glared into the flames.

He gulped down a cup of coffee, then he cut himself a plug of tobacco and shoved it into the right corner of his mouth, sucking on it angrily. How had Nicole Tyler managed to elude them?

No, it made no sense, whatsoever. How could someone who was born and bred into the genteel life of the rich in St. Louis manage to keep herself alive out there in the wild? Why, he doubted she even knew how to shoot a gun, much less defend herself.

"I just don't understand it," Sam said aloud, drawing the attention of the other men his way. "Where the hell can that tiny thing be? We've looked in every nook and cranny, except . . ."

"The mountain," Ace said, finishing Sam's sentence. "We've avoided goin' on that mountain. Maybe it's 'bout time, don't you think, Sam?"

Tom spoke up quickly, arguing against the suggestion. "Look at the color of those leaves on the aspens," he said, nodding toward a stand of aspens nearby. "Yeller. They're damn yeller. Don't that tell you somethin'? Don't it say that winter is not far behind? I wouldn't want to be stranded on that mountain when the snows set in. And then there's those damn Navaho. Chief Eagle Wolf would have all of our scalps, don'cha know? He and his warriors protect that mountain like it's made of gold!"

"Oh, shut up," Sam slammed right back at Tom. "You make me want to puke. I ain't never seen such a coward as you. If you weren't so good with a gun, I'd never have asked you to ride with me and the others. I depend on a quick trigger finger, and by gum, you've got the best. But I don't like the yellow side you show too often. Get a grip on yourself, Tom. Prove to us for a change that you're a man, not a dog with its tail tucked between its legs."

"Those are fightin' words," Tom said, as he jumped to his feet and glared down at Sam.

"Well, then, if'n it's a fight you want, you've chosen the right man," Sam said, himself leaping to his feet.

He spat a trail of tobacco juice over his right shoulder, some of it landing on his red plaid shirt, soiling it even more.

He then took a step closer to Tom and glared at him. "Put up your dukes," he growled out. "Now let's just see how much of a man you are. Are you going to fight, or are you all talk?"

Tom paled and stepped back away from Sam.

"Sam, you know I was only pullin' yore leg," he said, his voice drawn. "Come on now. Let's get back to what we should be discussin'. We shouldn't be fightin' 'mongst ourselves. We'll not gain anything by doin' that."

"Then shet yore mouth, you dumb bumpkin, and sit right down and behave yoreself," Sam said.

Sam lowered himself back down beside the fire, ignoring the stares of the other men.

"Give me a plate of that jackrabbit meat," he demanded, thrusting his tin plate close to Ace, who reached over to the spit above the fire and used his knife to cut more meat from the carcass.

Sam took the plate, spat out the tobacco, then with his fingers reached for a piece of the meat and shoved it into his mouth as he looked from man to man. "She couldn't jest disappear into thin air," he said while chewing. "She must be somewheres. Today, gents, we'll find 'er. I bet yore bottom dollar we'll find 'er."

"Dead or alive?" Ace asked, lifting an eyebrow as he spat the juice of his tobacco into the fire, causing sparks to fly in all directions.

"If'n we're lucky, she'll be alive," Sam said, frowning at Ace.

Ace frowned right back at him. "If'n we're lucky, we'll find her dead and then we can git back to playin' poker," he said. "I didn't join up with you to hunt down some gal that ain't never done me no harm. Sam, I wish'd you jest let this go. I'm itchin' to play a hand of cards. Now tell the truth. Ain't you?"

"I bet your bottom dollar the Injuns got 'er," Tom said, laughing throatily. "Now, wouldn't you jist love to see that flame-colored hair hangin' from the chief's scalp pole? Sam, as I see it, you might as well kiss the plan of having her yourself good-bye."

Sam glared at Tom. "You don't give up, do you? Shut yore trap," he growled. "I'll find her. She's going to pay for her father's crimes as her ma and pa have already paid."

Sam paused, wiped his mouth with the back of a hand, then frowned from man to man. "Listen well, gents," he growled. "I'll never give up lookin' for 'er. Killing Nicole is my final revenge against her damn gambler father. I won't rest until she's dead. She was her father's 'little princess,' his pride and joy. And she had the nerve to think she was too good for the likes of me. Well, when ol' Sam gets finished with her, she'll not be fit to be anyone's pride and joy. Actually, after we all get through with her, she'll welcome her death."

"I wish you'd listen to reason. We'd best not stick around here for much longer," Ace grumbled. "I'd hate to think of gettin' caught up in a snowstorm. We ain't familiar with surviving snow in this mountainous area."

"I'll worry about that, if, or when, it happens," Sam said tightly. "Right now my only concern is finding the wench. And we will find her before the weather turns. Then we can hightail it outta this area and go back to good ol' St. Louie where the pickings are good. We always know the best gambling houses and can spot a mark at a mere glance. Yep. Gents, the fun is just ahead of us. But for now, let's not miss out on the fun we can have with that little ol' gal."

"If'n you can guarantee we'll not get caught up here in the snow, I'm game, Sam," Tom said, then chuckled. "When we spot the wench all alone on her horse, it'll be like when we chased down that jackrabbit this mornin'. It didn't have a chance in hell of gettin' away from us."

"The difference is, Tom," Ace said dryly, "we clubbed that critter to death. We'll be just a mite gentler with the lady."

They all fell into a fit of laughter, except for Sam, who was picturing just how pretty Nicole Tyler was. He could not help thinking it was a waste, for he was not going to have any mercy when he found her.

There that pretty thing was, born only to die a death no pretty woman should have to endure.

But she wasn't just any woman. She was the daughter of the man who had been his most hated enemy.

It was only right that she join her pa in hell!

Chapter Twenty

The wind whispered soft and low through the yellow leaves of the aspen trees that stood close to where Eagle Wolf and his warriors sat on their horses. Like falling rain, the leaves seemed to murmur quietly.

Eagle Wolf and his warriors had just arrived at a bluff from which they could see much of the countryside below them.

Eagle Wolf's eyes narrowed as he gazed down at the Mormon community that he had seen more than once during his travels. Today his interest was spiked as he wondered whether Nicole might not have sought shelter there.

He had always been impressed when he saw how industrious the Mormons were. They planted many crops, corn, beans, squash, and other vegetables. They also had sheep and other animals he had heard were called cows.

He knew from having sheep at his stronghold that they were used for food, and also for clothing after the sheep's wool was removed from them.

As for the cow animals, he had learned that

they produced a delicious white drink called milk and something else called butter.

The Mormon women all dressed alike, in long, plain cotton garb. They had no decoration on any of their long dresses such as the Navaho women loved having on their clothes.

All of the Mormon women's skin was pale, and their hair was worn atop their heads, wound and secured to form some sort of knot.

These women were nothing like Nicole. He would never forget her loose, flaming red hair, or her face, which was so beautiful, especially when he caught her in a blush.

He had never known anyone like her, and doubted that he ever would again.

He could see people coming and going in the town, but he saw no children anywhere, and that puzzled him. The sun was warm in the sky this late autumn day, the sky was blue, with fluffy white clouds floated past overhead. The air was sweet with the aroma of autumn flowers that he saw growing over the ground, the color of those flowers as beautiful as their scent.

Why would the children not be outside playing in this sunshine and sweet air?

He knew that the Navaho children would be out now, busy at their games. He smiled as he thought of how the braves enjoyed foot and pony races while the girls enjoyed playing house.

He hoped to have his own children to watch and enjoy someday. He suddenly envisioned a son born in both his and Nicole's images. A boy with long, black hair, and grass green eyes.

He wondered, though, about whether his Navaho people would accept such a child.

He shook his head to clear his thoughts and again focused on why he had left the safety of his village on this beautiful autumn day.

Nicole!

Suddenly the sound of a bell ringing echoed up to him and his warriors, and he spotted a building that sat in the center of the small community.

He had heard of white people's schoolhouses and believed that this might be one.

Or was it a place of worship? Did a church not also have a bell at the top of the building?

His eyes narrowed again when he recalled that Nicole had spoken about wanting to be a teacher. She had even attended a special sort of school in order to be able to teach children.

Although he had already guessed from the way she spoke and behaved that Nicole was a woman of much intelligence, it had been even more impressive to know that she was a woman with an education that none of his Navaho people had, or ever would have.

His heart raced at the thought that Nicole might have found her way to this community. When these people realized that she was a teacher, would they not have invited her to stay, to teach their children?

Eagle Wolf smiled as he imagined the petite flame-haired woman standing before the classroom. He knew about classrooms and teachers from a scout who had once spied through a schoolhouse window to see just what this teaching was all about.

His scout, Two Birds, had brought his newfound knowledge back to Eagle Wolf and explained to him all about a black sort of board that was on the wall of the schoolhouse, and how the woman teacher there used a small white object to make letters on that blackboard.

Two Birds had even stayed long enough to listen to the children sing beautiful songs, quite different from the Navaho's songs and ways of singing them.

Two Birds had frowned at one thing that he had seen . . . an American flag that stood at the front of the room. It had been a sore reminder of the emblem that white soldiers carried with them into battle.

When his scout had heard the arrival of horses at the front of the schoolhouse, he had fled. He had hurried back to his people and directly to Eagle Wolf with his report.

Having heard firsthand about the schoolhouse and how fascinating it was, Eagle Wolf had wanted to see it, himself, but he had not dared go there for fear of not being as lucky as his scout.

If he were caught spying through a window, surely his enemies would not hesitate to hang him without even questioning why he was there. Curiosity would surely not have been an excuse they would have accepted.

Ever since he had sat and listened to Two Birds talking about this school and the blackboard with white markings on it, Eagle Wolf had secretly longed to have the same for his people's children.

But he had fought off those longings, for he knew the impossibility of giving this special gift to the Navaho children.

That had not stopped him from thinking that having a white man's education could benefit his people in so many ways. Knowledge.

Ho, knowledge of all the things taught the children in the white people's schoolhouses could take his Navaho children into adulthood with many ways to fight back when confronted by greedy whites. No one would then cheat the Owl Clan with trickster papers as the Navaho had been cheated before.

While Eagle Wolf had sat with Nicole beside the campfire, he had actually envisioned her among his people, teaching their children. He had planned to ask her this favor on the morning that he woke up and found her gone.

His heart skipped a beat when he spotted children running from the schoolhouse building. His heart sped up when someone else stepped from the schoolhouse, too. Even at this distance he could recognize Nicole's flame red hair.

He could not deny the feeling of relief that washed through him. At this very moment, he knew that she was his destiny. And he would not allow anything to stand in the way of their future together.

He turned to his warriors. "Dismount," he said flatly. "I have found the woman. We will wait for night to fall, and then I will find a way to go to Nicole and tell her that we have come for her. We will take her back to our stronghold, where she will be safe, forever."

"But the woman is safe now," said one of the warriors. Striped Wing was puzzled by his chief's persistence concerning this woman whose skin was white.

It was true that she was beautiful, her flaming red hair fascinating also to Striped Wing. But the fact remained that she was white, and white people had taken so much from the Navaho. How could any Navaho warrior want to share his life with someone of that skin color?

"It might seem so, but I do not believe she is happy there," Eagle Wolf said. "Being safe is not everything. I must at least go and speak with her. And then I will know if what I believe is true, or false."

"You will chance everything in order to get that answer?" Striped Wing dared to ask.

"It is not for you to question, but to follow, and do as your chief tells you," Eagle Wolf said in a way that he hoped would not be too hurtful to his warrior. He knew that Striped Wing was only thinking as most Navaho would think.

Right now the safety of one woman surpassed all else in Eagle Wolf's mind, for she was his heart, his very being!

"Chief Eagle Wolf, I understand what you are saying, but—" Striped Wing dared to say, stopping when Eagle Wolf interrupted him.

"I will go and speak with her tonight," Eagle Wolf said flatly. "So do not waste any more words arguing with your chief. I am just not certain how safe she is with those people, for I know little of the habits of Mormons. All I wish to know is that she is content. I will soon go to her and ask her how happy she is. If she answers the way I believe she will answer me, I will then ask her to leave with us."

"And if she refuses?" Striped Wing asked blandly.

Eagle Wolf did not openly respond to that question, but he knew that if Nicole refused to leave with him, he would be lonely for her, forever!

Chapter Twenty-one

Dreading having to leave this haven that had been offered her by these gentle Mormon people, Nicole paced the floor of the cute home that she had been given as her very own.

But she knew that her occupation of that house was to be only for a short time if Jeremiah Schrock had anything to say about it. He expected her to be so grateful for his kindness that she would actually marry him, and make him that third wife the children spoke of so eagerly.

"A brother," she whispered, shuddering at the thought.

Even though I must go, I dread leaving, she thought, tears filling her eyes at the thought of being all alone again out where she knew there were dangers everywhere.

If she was not attacked by men like Sam Partain and his gang, then there were the animals that roamed, both day and night, in search of food.

She recalled seeing one particular wolf more than once, as it skulked nearby, almost hidden behind thick brush.

She knew it was the same animal because there was an identifying mark where bare skin was exposed on its side.

She still couldn't understand why that wolf hadn't pounced on her when it was so close. And it was strange how the wolf would suddenly appear, then in one blink of Nicole's eyes, disappear again.

It seemed as though the wolf was looking for someone in particular, or something. She was glad that apparently she was of no interest to the creature.

It was such a mystical being, Nicole even now felt a shiver race her spine to think about it.

Anyhow, no matter whether there were evil men out there searching for her, or a mystical wolf, Nicole had no choice but to leave the Mormon community.

And she would.

Tonight.

After the lamps were blown out in each house and everything but the moon's glow was dark, she would leave.

"Yes, I must escape," she whispered as she went to a mirror on the wall and gazed at her reflection.

Her hair was brushed until it shone. Her face was shining and fresh from a washing only moments ago.

The rims of her eyes were slightly red. More than once this evening she had not been able to keep from crying at the thought of the danger that lay ahead.

But now she had one other thing to do.

She knew that she must be the only one who had not visited the large dining hall for the evening meal.

She had watched the families entering the building in groups. Her front windows faced so that she could see the dining hall, and now the lamplight streamed from the building, and she could hear the sound of voices.

She was afraid to join the others for the meal, for fear that they would somehow read her mind and know what she had planned. Nicole hesitated to take her shawl from its peg on the wall, thinking that perhaps she could get away with not going there tonight.

But she knew better.

If she didn't show up, Jeremiah would most certainly come to check on her. Already, he was strangely possessive of her.

As she grabbed her shawl and placed it around her shoulders, she realized how much her fingers were trembling. She would have to get hold of herself if she was to get through these next moments without anyone being the wiser as to what caused her nervousness.

Escape!

Yes, she had to make certain no one realized what she was planning.

If there was even an inkling of suspicion, Jeremiah would lock her in the cabin tonight.

Sighing heavily, Nicole stepped out into the dusk of early evening.

She shivered when the air brushed against her face. The evenings were cool now that autumn was soon to fade away and turn into the coldness of winter.

That, alone, should be a deterrent to what she had planned. But she had to believe that before winter set in, she would find a place where she could live safely and put all the ugliness of these past days from her mind.

She stopped and inhaled a nervous breath as she came to the steps that led up to the dining hall. She didn't have time to take many breaths, for Jeremiah suddenly emerged from the building. Smiling, he held a hand outstretched before him.

"I thought you would never come," Jeremiah said, taking Nicole by the hand even though she tried to pull it away. "I imagine you were resting after your first day of teaching. I expect it was quite tiring. Was it, Nicole?"

"Yes, very," Nicole said softly.

She hated that his hand still held her own, as though she belonged to him. He led her into the large building, as though she was his trophy for everyone to see.

She was very aware of how everyone turned

and gazed at her as Jeremiah took her to the table, where she was made to sit between him and one of his children, Kathryn. Nicole found that quite peculiar, for she knew the children usually ate away from their parents at another table.

Yet as she looked quickly around her, she noticed that all of the children were at their parents' tables tonight.

She suddenly realized that there was something else unusual about the meal. A cake with burning candles sat in the center of the main table.

She wondered whose birthday it was.

"Surprise!" the children suddenly boomed out as they jumped to their feet so that they could see Nicole better.

"What?" Nicole gasped, her shawl falling away from her shoulders and onto her chair. "It's not . . . my . . . birthday."

"Well, no, it's not," Jeremiah said, drawing Nicole's eyes quickly to him. "This was the first day of your teaching our children. We are all so happy to have you, especially the children, we felt that we needed to have a celebration of sorts, with you the person of honor."

"Truly?" Nicole said, stunned by the sweetness of what these people had done for her.

She looked around her at the smiling faces of the children, and guilt spread through her with a strange coldness.

How could she leave these children when she knew just how happy they were to have her there?

"I don't know what to say," she gulped out.

She was terribly conflicted now about what she had planned to do. If it meant so much to the children that she was there, how on earth could she disappoint them by leaving after she had taught school for only one day?

Jeremiah fetched the cake, then placed it in front of Nicole on the table. "I know it might be strange for you to have candles on a cake when it is not your birthday," he said. "But as I said, in a sense, it is your birthday. It is a birthday for all of our children. That is how much having a teacher means to them. We are truly established now in our new settlement, because we have a teacher. And you are a part of our community, too, even though you are not of Mormon faith."

"But she will be!" the children chimed in, almost in the same breath. "We shall teach her about our faith as she teaches us our reading and mathematical skills."

That made the color drain from Nicole's face. She hadn't even thought about becoming a Mormon, but wouldn't Jeremiah expect her to be a woman of his faith if she was to be his wife?

Now, no matter that these children had welcomed her so wonderfully with a cake and candles, she knew she must leave.

She must escape tonight!

Jeremiah slid the cake back to the center of the table. "We'll cut the cake after we have all eaten the main meal," he said as the children

scrambled to go and sit now at their usual assigned table.

Several men came and took the empty chairs
away, and then women began bringing the bowls
of food into the room. The smell of fried chicken
filled the room.

Nicole scarcely tasted any of the food as she
forced herself to eat. She almost gagged on each
bite as she thought ahead to what she must do.

Even the corn on the cob, which was dripping
with delicious freshly churned butter, had no fla-
vor whatsoever to Nicole. It was as though all of
her taste buds had been removed because of her
fear and anxiety.

Through the entire meal, Nicole felt Jeremiah's
eyes on her, as well as Nancy's and Martha's. It
must be plain to all that she was the object of Jeremiah's affection and the women's resentment.

Yes, she must leave.

But another problem hit her like a slap in the
face when she recognized that the man across the
table from her was one of the sentries who
guarded the community.

How would she get around him and the others
without their seeing her? How would she keep
from being caught by Jeremiah?

Chapter Twenty-two

The smell of roasted meat lay heavy in the air as the campfire shot sparks heavenward from the grease dripping into the flames.

Sam Partain was too restless to sit and idly chat with his friends. He paced back and forth while ignoring the complaints of his men, who said that he was driving them wild by acting so nervous.

But Sam couldn't stop his brain from thinking about Nicole and the fact that they had found no sign of her on the mountain today.

He and his friends had split up, covering much of the land where she could possibly have gotten on horseback, but they'd had no luck. That only meant to him that someone was giving her sanctuary.

His mind kept wandering back to that Mormon community. There was something suspicious about the way that one Mormon took over and spoke for the rest of the group. The fellow had said that no young woman had come there. But while that man had been talking, Sam had studied the faces of the women who appeared at the doors of their homes, or in the large garden, in the midst of their autumn harvest.

He had most certainly not seen Nicole among those women. But if she *had* been there, she might have gone quickly into hiding.

Had he been lied to?

He went and sat down on a blanket before the fire, his mind made up. "I've got to go back there," he blurted out, drawing all eyes to him.

"Where?" Ace asked.

"To that damn Mormon community, that's where," Sam said, his voice filled with anger that Nicole had eluded him so successfully thus far.

"Why on earth would you go back there and pester those innocent people?" Tom asked, his eyes narrowing angrily. "Sam, I have understood this thing about Nicole, and I've been willing to help you find her, but why must you go back to that community? They've never done anything to you. Let 'em be, Sam. Let 'em be."

"I don't believe they are all so innocent," Sam growled out. "I remember something in that man's eyes when he told me he'd not seen Nicole. It was the look of a man who is lying. That's what I seen. I've got to go back there and figure out just what he was lying about. Then we'll make 'em all pay for what he's done."

"I don't want no part of it," Ace said, scrambling to his feet. "I don't want no part of any of this anymore. I'm itchin' to play poker. Sam, let's just go on to St. Louis and find us a game. Let Nicole be.

Don't you know that sooner or later you'll run across her again? Get your vengeance then. Not now. Let's go, Sam, tomorrow, to St. Louis."

"If that's what you want, no one is stoppin' you," Sam said tightly. "Go on. Git. But don't expect me ever to loan you any more money once you've lost all of your own gambling."

"Oh, Sam, why can't you listen to reason?" Ace whined. He sat back down, lowering his eyes. "I'm stayin'. Whatever you feel you need to do, I'll help."

"That's more like it," Sam said, reaching over and patting Ace on the shoulder.

He laughed throatily. "I think that meat is ready to eat," he said. "Ace, git me a piece and don't be slow about it."

He stretched his long, lean legs out before him as he took the chunk of meat from Ace, bit off a huge hunk and started chewing it.

"Yep, tomorrow I'll pay those Mormon people another visit," he said, while chewing. He looked around at his men. "None of you have to play a role in this. You'll stay hidden whilst I do the dirty work."

"You're not going to harm any of them if you don't get the answers you want?" Tom asked, chewing on his own meat.

"We'll just have to wait and see 'bout that, won't we?" Sam said, idly shrugging.

He laughed, almost choking on the meat in his mouth.

He then gazed slowly around at his men. "I've got to fess up," he said, his eyes dancing with teasing. "I lied to you moments ago. You see, I ain't going to that place alone at all. You are going with me. It'll take more than me to search that place to make certain Nicole ain't there."

He laughed again as the men groaned and moaned after learning what was expected of them.

Tom didn't groan or moan. He just stared angrily at Sam, who ignored him, apparently lost in thought about tomorrow.

"Sam, surely you don't mean what you just said," Tom finally blurted out. "Tell us you are just joshin' us. I don't want to do it, Sam. I'm sure the rest don't neither."

"If'n you ever want to be with me again at a poker table, draggin' in the coins like we always do, you'd best not say another thing against what I plan to do," Sam warned. "Do I make myself clear enough?"

Tom didn't respond. He just yanked off another bite of meat and chewed on it, his eyes now gazing into the flames of the fire, somehow seeing the redheaded wench there, smiling flirtatiously at him.

Suddenly it didn't seem all that wrong, what Sam had planned for that wench, for Tom would surely have a part of 'er, too, before killin' her.

He smiled at the thought of touching her soft,

pink flesh, then rolling her beneath him and doing what he had not done for so long.

Yep, he'd go with Sam after all, if it meant having a piece of that young thing as he had himself a piece of this meat he was still chewin' on.

Chapter Twenty-three

The moon seemed to be the only light left in the Mormon community as Nicole looked from her window, checking to see if she saw any lamplight in any of the other windows. She sighed when she saw none.

This was the opportunity that she had been waiting for ever since she had returned to her house after finishing the evening meal. She had packed her things in her travel bag, had changed into warmer clothes for her night out in the open, and was now ready to make her escape.

Wearing a warm, lined jacket, she grabbed up her travel bag, in which she had shoved the barrel end of her rifle. Slowly, she opened the door, hoping it would not squeak.

She was in luck. There was not any sound at all.

The only thing she could hear now were the songs of the crickets, which seemed to get weaker as each night passed. She remembered back in St. Louis, how the chilly nights of autumn seemed to numb the songs right out of the crickets that she had enjoyed hearing all summer long.

She stopped and winced when she heard the yipping of a wolf. Its call of the wild was way too close for comfort.

Was this the same wolf she'd seen before? Or was it possibly another one that might be more aggressive?

She knew that she must get a grip on herself and be on her way. The longer she stayed in the Mormon community, the closer she came to being made Jeremiah's wife.

She shuddered at the thought of that man touching her.

That thought gave her the courage to hurry onward. The very idea of marrying Jeremiah Schrock brought a sick feeling to the pit of her stomach. He was a deceitful man.

He had deceived her into believing that he was genuinely concerned about her, when all along he just wanted a woman he could coerce into being his third wife.

"Never," she whispered to herself.

She moved cautiously away from the house, keeping alert for any movement in the night. She knew there were sentries posted in several strategic places in order to keep the community safe from the likes of Sam Partain and his men.

She was glad when she reached the corral where her horse was kept. She tiptoed into the corral and located the saddles that were stored in a small shed at its edge.

She grabbed a saddle and soon had her horse ready except for the travel bag that sat waiting to be tied to its back. After that was done, she took up the reins and led her mare through the gate, securing it behind her.

She cringed when one of the horses in the corral gave a loud whinny. Nicole stopped quickly.

She looked in all directions, praying to herself that no one had heard the sound. Thank goodness she saw no one, nor any lamp being suddenly lighted.

Everyone seemed to be fast asleep. She prayed they would stay asleep until she made her way into the shadows of the aspen forest that stretched away from the village on one side.

Her heart pounding, her knees weak from fear, Nicole kept walking her horse through the small community. She breathed a deep sigh of relief when she was finally outside its perimeters, standing with her mare in the shadows of the forest, where the moon's glow was not able to penetrate the yellowing leaves overhead.

"We made it," she whispered as she stroked her mount's gray-speckled mane. "Now let's get going."

She had just put her foot into the stirrup when she heard a noise behind her. She stiffened and dropped her foot back to the ground when she realized what that noise was.

The snapping of a twig. Someone was close by.

She tried to mount the horse again, but jumped in terror when a hand came out of the darkness and grabbed her wrist.

She was turned quickly around and found herself face-to-face with one of the men appointed sentry tonight.

It was Jacob Jones.

"Please unhand me, Jacob," Nicole begged, struggling and yanking as she tried to get free of his grip. "Please let me leave. I love the children and would love to be their teacher, but I learned today that Jeremiah Schrock plans to take me as his third wife. Jacob, I don't want to marry Jeremiah. I could never be a third wife to any man, especially a man I could never love."

Jacob gently dropped his hand from her wrist, allowing Nicole to step away from him.

"Nicole, I am not standing guard to keep you in, but to keep the evil men out," Jacob said in a gentle voice.

Nicole could barely see his eyes. But she remembered that they were a striking blue color and always showed such kindness in them.

She also recalled his thin face, where reddish whiskers grew into a neatly trimmed beard. And as usual, he wore black, which blended into the darkness of night.

"Nicole, I will not force you to stay, but I fear for your safety if you leave. You know those evil men are looking for you," Jacob continued in his soft voice. "You know they have no good intentions toward you."

"I am very aware of those men and what their intentions are toward me," Nicole said softly. "Sam Partain killed my parents, and I don't believe that Sam Partain will stop until he finds and kills me, too."

"Yet you will risk his finding you rather than stay here where you will be safe and well cared for?" Jacob said, his voice revealing how surprised he was at her choice. "Jeremiah has made Nancy and Martha a good husband. He would also be kind and caring to you. He has prayed often for a son. He believes you would bear him not only one, but many."

"And that is exactly why I must take my chances against Sam Partain," Nicole softly argued. "I don't want to marry any man that I don't love, and I don't want a man marrying me only to bear him sons."

"That marriage would bring much happiness into your life," Jacob said in a pleading way. "The women of our community are very happy. I have never seen any of them cry. Nicole, you could be happy here, too. If you blessed Jeremiah with a son, he would never stop repaying you. Gifts, Nicole. You would be given gifts you cannot even imagine."

"I want no gifts, I want no favors, I only want my freedom and the right to fall in love with whom I want to love. I would never be content with the life that is offered me by Jeremiah," Nicole responded. "Now, Jacob, I am going to ride away from this community. The only way you can stop me is to shoot me. And I know that you wouldn't do that. You are a man of God, a man of good heart. I just hope that Jeremiah doesn't hold it against you too much that you let me go."

"He is a man of God and he will accept God's bidding if it is for you to be on your way and find happiness elsewhere," Jacob said softly. He held the rifle tightly at his side. "Go, Nicole. Do what your heart tells you to do, and God bless."

Nicole was so stunned that Jacob was actuallly letting her go, she stood there for a moment, staring at him. Then she went to him and flung herself into his arms.

"Thank you," she softly cried. "Oh, Jacob, thank you for your sweet kindness."

She felt his arm tighten around her.

She tensed, realizing at that moment he could actually lock his arms around her and force her to walk with him back into the village.

But to her relief, he was truly the kind man that she thought him to be. He released his arms from around her waist and stepped back.

"Jacob, oh, Jacob, will you be punished for allowing me to leave?" she asked, truly afraid for the kindhearted man.

"Jeremiah is a good man," Jacob said, smiling at Nicole. "He would never mistreat a brother. Go, Nicole. Be safe. And when you find the man you can love, I hope you will find much happiness as his wife."

She wanted to tell him that she had already found that man, and that she truly felt he was her destiny. But she knew that neither Jacob nor Jeremiah would ever understand how she could love an Indian. Most whites, even the kindhearted Mormons, saw Indians as savages.

"I truly believe that I shall find that perfect man," Nicole said, putting a foot into the stirrup, and mounting her steed.

She gazed down at Jacob. "I shall never forget your kindness," she murmured. "Jacob, thank you. Thank you so much."

"I will not forget your brave heart," Jacob replied, then turned and walked away, while Nicole rode in the opposite direction into the darkness of the aspen forest.

Nicole sighed heavily. She knew that if it had been anyone but Jacob who'd found her, she would even now be back at the house that had been assigned her.

"Oh, Jeremiah, what are you going to do when you realize that I am gone?" she whispered into the wind.

She realized that he might come searching for her again.

She would not allow him to find her.

Chapter Twenty-four

Seeking the safety of the mountain, Nicole now rode up a narrow pass that was scarcely visible in the night.

She wasn't sure whether to thank the moon for being bright tonight, allowing her to see a few feet ahead of herself, or curse it for possibly making her visible to those who might be searching for her.

She hoped and prayed that at this time of night Sam Partain and his gang would already be settled in beside a campfire, having given up their search until tomorrow.

Her most ardent prayer was that Sam Partain had given up on finding her altogether. She knew the lure of the poker table for him. She doubted that Sam could stay away from it for long.

Her father had been cursed by the same compulsion. Perhaps in the end it would lead to Sam's death as well.

She forced her thoughts elsewhere, for thinking of Sam Partain and the parents he had taken from her would forever cause a pain she could not describe. For this moment, at least, she was safe from all men who threatened her.

She reached down and rested a hand on the butt end of the rifle shoved into her travel bag. Were she to need it quickly, it was there, ready and loaded.

She thought of her father and how proud he would be of the backbone and bravery she'd showed at a time in her life when only she could make things right again.

And then she thought of someone else.

Eagle Wolf.

If only she could see him again. If only he cared enough to search for her.

Could it be that he had decided not to accept her disappearance in his life and was out there even now searching for her? But no, he would surely be in his home, sitting leisurely beside his lodge fire, possibly having already eaten a delicious meal of whatever the Navaho ate. No doubt his mind was on anything but her.

Probably when he had awakened the other morning and found her gone, it was the last time he'd ever thought of her.

He had surely accepted that if she had fled from him in such a way, she wanted nothing more to do with him.

As she rode through another stand of aspens, Nicole welcomed the glimmer of their yellow leaves in the night as the moon fell upon them.

There was a peace that came with the rustling of their leaves.

The breeze picked up, and then she could scarcely see them because dark clouds suddenly covered the moon.

But she could still hear the leaves rustling, and suddenly did not feel so alone as she rode in the company of the trees and their lovely murmuring.

She closed her eyes for a moment and thought of times back home when she and her mother had walked hand in hand in a forest of cottonwood trees in the autumn. They, too, made the same sound, like a whisper of music.

Thinking of her sweet, precious mother brought a horrible ache to Nicole's heart. She was missing her mother so much at this moment, she could hardly stand it.

If only she could see her one more time.

If only she could hear her soft laughter.

She opened her eyes and felt suddenly faint when a horse came out of the shadows at her. The moon was still hidden, so she could not see who was on the horse.

But the man's voice, so deep and masculine, and oh, so wonderfully friendly and caring, revealed who the man was.

"Eagle Wolf!" she cried as the clouds slid away from the moon and suddenly revealed his sculpted, handsome face to her.

Never in her life had she been so relieved, so happy, to see anyone as she was to see Eagle Wolf.

Eagle Wolf, however, was not at all surprised to see her there on her horse. As soon as she had got free of the Mormon compound, he had trailed her, separating himself from his warriors and giving them the freedom to return to their homes and families tonight.

He no longer needed anyone to help him save the woman he loved.

He had waited to approach her because he was not certain how to come upon her in the night without giving her a terrible fright. But now that they were together, and he saw the relief on her face, he knew that he had done the right thing to search out this white woman, whose heart belonged to him, even though she might not yet realize it.

"How did you know where I was?" Nicole asked, searching his eyes.

"I saw you leaving the Mormon village," Eagle Wolf said, stopping his horse directly beside hers so that he could reach out and touch her.

But he waited to be sure she would accept such a touch. He must remember that she had chosen to flee him as he lay asleep beside the campfire.

"You . . . saw . . . me?" Nicole asked.

With his horse right next to her own, she found it hard to concentrate, much less carry on a normal conversation.

If he knew the effect that he had on her, he would understand how glad she was to see him. He would know that she loved him although they had not yet even shared a kiss.

"When I discovered that you had left while I slept, I was not certain what I should do," he explained. "I did not know why you had left. I wrestled with my feelings about whether or not to go after you. I decided to let you do what your heart had led you to do. I went to my home and tried to forget you. But . . ."

What he was actually confessing to Nicole made her almost melt in her saddle, for she now knew just how much this man loved her.

Oh, Lord, he felt the same way she did about him!

She wanted to reach out and plead with him to take her on his lap and embrace and kiss her. It took all of her willpower not to blurt out to him that she needed no more explanation, that she now understood his feelings.

"But . . . ?" she prompted at his awkward silence. "You were saying . . . ?"

"I was saying that I did not want to live without you," Eagle Wolf said, his voice drawn. "I am saying that I want you to go with me to my home and allow me to love and protect you, forever."

Nicole's face turned hot with a blush, for her inner excitement was almost too much to bear.

It was a sweet sort of pain that came from loving him and knowing that he loved her, too.

This man with the voice that stirred all of her inner emotions, this man with the boldest of dark eyes that made her almost swoon, truly did love her and want her.

"Why did you leave the safe shelter of the Mormon settlement?" he asked next. "Did you not know the danger of traveling alone?"

"There are all sorts of dangers to avoid and I just left one of the worst kind behind me," Nicole said, a sudden shiver going through her body at the thought of Jeremiah forcing her into his bed with him.

"What do you mean by that?" Eagle Wolf asked, leaning closer to her, yet still not taking her hand in his as he so badly wished to do. He never wanted her to be afraid of him.

"The danger that I avoided by leaving the Mormon community came from one man," Nicole said, her voice full of emotion.

"How so?" Eagle Wolf asked.

"Jeremiah Schrock found me and took me back to his community for only one reason," Nicole said. "He wanted to make me his third wife. Yet there is more than that. He . . . he . . . wanted me to bear him sons, something his other two wives had not been able to give him."

Eagle Wolf had heard about how Mormon men took more than one wife, so he was not surprised at this news, but it still angered him. This white man had tricked Nicole into believing that he was rescuing her, while all along, he had an ulterior motive for taking her to his home.

Eagle Wolf also wanted to marry Nicole, but he would never entice her to his home with tricks. He never wanted anything but truth between them, for he knew that she was the sort of woman who hated tricks and lies as much as he.

Yet he still had to ask her, for he had learned many lessons in life, and one was never to take anyone, or anything, for granted.

"I understand why you fled the Mormon settlement," Eagle Wolf said, a note of caution in his voice. "If you accept my invitation to return to my stronghold, would you flee again as you have twice before? The first time, you ran away from a man who had your best interests at heart; the second time from one with selfish needs. Could you be happy in my home? I left the safety of my stronghold to search for you in the Mormon settlement. I was waiting for darkness, and then I was going to enter the settlement without anyone knowing that I was there. You are the only reason I would take such a risk."

"How did you know that I was there in the first place?" Nicole asked.

"I spotted the Mormon town from the mountain. While I was watching, I saw you leave the schoolhouse after many children," Eagle Wolf said.

"And you waited until it was dark to come to me," Nicole said.

She then blurted out, "Eagle Wolf, did you not know the dangers in doing that? There are many men standing guard all around the town. Had you been caught, I cannot say what they would have done to you."

She lowered her eyes, then quickly raised them again and gazed intently into his. "You risked everything for me," she murmured. "You care that much for me?"

"I care that much for you," he affirmed. "I see in your eyes that you also care for me. I am right, aren't I?"

"Yes, you are right," Nicole said, again feeling as though her insides were melting. He took one of her hands in his and kissed it, then released it again and grabbed his reins.

"I know that you are puzzling over how quickly we have fallen in love, but in life, it is best not to question such things. Just accept our good fortune and be happy for what your God and my Great Spirit have given us," Eagle Wolf said, his heart soaring to know that he had been right about Nicole, that she did care for him.

She had surely fled him out of fear of what his people might feel about their chief bringing a white woman home with him.

"My mother read the Bible often," Nicole murmured. "One thing Mother taught me was that the good Lord sometimes takes away, but He also gives back. My parents were taken from me, but now God has blessed me with knowing you."

"Will you go with me to my home?" Eagle Wolf asked, searching her eyes, which were suddenly wet with tears. "I owe you a debt because you cared for me when I was ill. I would like to repay this debt by taking you where you will always be safe."

Nicole wiped the happy tears from her eyes, then smiled and nodded.

"Yes," she said softly. "Oh, yes, Eagle Wolf, please take me to your home."

For a moment, she thought about his people, and how they might react when they saw her enter their stronghold. But she quickly cast that concern aside.

Eagle Wolf was their chief. He had the right to do whatever he pleased.

Eagle Wolf badly wanted to reach for her and kiss her, but he did not want to rush into anything that might cause her to doubt the sincerity of his offer of sanctuary. He did not want her to think that he had any other motive for taking her home and offering to protect her.

Of course, he hoped in time that she would agree to become his wife. He believed that, deep down inside herself, she understood his desire and accepted it.

He believed she was willing to share her life with him, for had she not as much as told him so?

He did not want her to compare his kindness

toward her to Jeremiah Schrock's, and perhaps think he wanted her only to bear him a son.

He did want a son, but he wanted Nicole even more than any child that might be born of their love!

Chapter Twenty-five

The morning sun wafted through the windows of the large dining hall at the Mormon settlement. Oatmeal was being ladled into bowls along the children's table, where they sat waiting for everyone to start eating. Meanwhile, Jeremiah fidgeted nervously on his seat between his two wives, his gaze moving often now to the door that led into the building.

Nicole was the only one who had not yet arrived for breakfast.

Jeremiah saw that even the children had begun to notice her empty chair, casting quick glances over their shoulders toward it. He could hear how quiet the children had become in their uneasiness at her absence.

He knew how eager they were to attend school again today. They not only loved learning things, but also had grown quickly to love their pretty, young teacher whose smile would brighten any room.

Tired of wondering about Nicole, and why she had not arrived for breakfast, Jeremiah shoved his chair back and stood quickly. Although he saw the frown both his wives gave him, he strode from the building.

As he stepped outside, he found himself surrounded by many horsemen, who had arrived quietly without anyone being the wiser.

Jeremiah recognized one of them. It was none other than the man who had come questioning about Nicole.

Jeremiah swallowed hard and took a slow step backward, yet he knew that trying to escape inside the building would be both cowardly and futile. His heart pounded inside his chest.

He could not help trembling when the man he recognized from his long blond hair and devilish eyes dismounted his steed and came to stand directly in front of Jeremiah. His eyes were no more friendly than Jeremiah remembered their being the last time they had come face-to-face.

Then Jeremiah thought of something that made him grow cold inside.

The sentries! What had happened to them? Why had they sounded no alarm?

He looked past Sam Partain and fought back the urge to vomit. Thomas Hayden lay dead on the ground, blood spattered across his chest.

It was apparent that he had not been shot there, or the report of the gun would have been heard. He had surely been shot at his sentry post, and been brought from there. The body had been dropped on the ground, as though it were worthless.

Jeremiah looked quickly at Sam again and shivered when he saw a slow, mocking smile lift the corners of his mouth.

"You killed them all, didn't you?" Jeremiah asked, anger now taking the place of shock and despair at seeing such a God-fearing family man downed heartlessly while trying to protect his community.

"I'm the one who'll be askin' the questions," Sam said tightly. "Not you. You'll be the one answering them. Now tell me, Mormon, where is Nicole Tyler? You'd best tell me, or you're the next one to get a bullet in the gut."

Jeremiah knew that the only way he could possibly protect the rest of his people was to cooperate with the evil-eyed murderer. Yes, he must give Nicole up so that the rest of his friends might live. She would be the sacrificial lamb.

The only thing that worried him was the fact that she hadn't arrived at the dining hall for breakfast. What had caused the delay?

Perhaps she had just awakened later than she had planned and was even now dressing as fast as she could.

"If Nicole Tyler is the reason that you and your men have returned to this community, then you can have her," Jeremiah said stiffly, filled with guilt at what he was doing.

But his people and their safety must come first.

He could find another woman one of these days to take Nicole's place in his life.

He doubted, though, that he would find a schoolmarm as talented as Nicole, especially one whom the children loved at once as they had loved Nicole.

"So I was right, huh?" Sam said. He grabbed Jeremiah quickly by his collar and yanked him closer so that their faces were only inches apart. "She was here all along, wasn't she? I knew it. I don't know why I let you bamboozle me when I was here the last time. Well, this time you'd best give 'er up to me, do you hear? Don't try any pranks on me. Take me to that woman now, or I swear, I'll plug a hole in your belly so quick you won't know what happened."

"Promise me first that you won't harm anyone else in Hope," Jeremiah choked out.

Jeremiah's face was hot and he was having a hard time breathing because of Sam's stranglehold on his throat. He breathed much more easily when Sam's hand slipped away.

"I won't promise you nothin'," Sam growled out. "Jist take me to her. Then I'll let you know what my plans are for you and the rest of these Mormons."

"For God's Sake, have mercy on the rest of these innocent people," Jeremiah pleaded as Sam released him.

Jeremiah stumbled backward, yet his eyes were still locked in a silent war with Sam.

"If you must kill someone, let it be only me," Jeremiah then said. "Leave everyone else alive. These people deserve to live. They are God's chosen!"

"Hogwash," Sam said, chuckling. He nodded to his men. "Stay here and keep an eye on things, but only shoot if you are threatened."

He laughed mockingly. "Leave anyone who doesn't cause you trouble," he said. "We can't harm God's chosen, now, can we?"

Fear and anger overwhelmed Jeremiah as Sam gave him a hard shove, then followed along as Jeremiah headed for the house that had been assigned to Nicole.

When they reached Nicole's house, Jeremiah stopped and gave Sam a pleading look in a last effort to change the evil man's mind.

Nicole did not deserve what this man surely had planned for her. Jeremiah did not even want to think about it.

He felt responsible for the woman's plight, and he did not see how even he could get out of this situation without dying.

"Go on in and be sure not to alert her that I'm here, comin' in behind you," Sam said. He motioned with his rifle toward the closed door. "If you try anything at all, just remember that I have my finger on the trigger, and believe me, it loves pullin' triggers."

"Please, please don't do this," Jeremiah pleaded one last time with the madman.

"You are one inch away from suckin' in your last gulp of air," Sam growled out. "Open that door. Step inside. I'll be right behind you."

Jeremiah swallowed hard, grabbed hold of the doorknob, then slowly turned it.

When he finally got the door open, he gasped when he saw that Nicole's bed had not been slept in. With a quick look around him, he saw that all of Nicole's belongings were gone.

"She's gone," he said, turning and gazing in terror at Sam as he came into the house. "Everything she had with her is gone. She must've left in the middle of the night. She must've not liked teaching the children."

Sam shoved him aside so hard, Jeremiah fell to his knees on the floor. He crawled away from Sam as the gunman stood there, looking slowly around the room.

"Well, she is certainly gone," Sam said, idly scratching his brow with his free hand.

He swung around and glared at Jeremiah.

He took a step closer and kicked him so that Jeremiah fell clumsily on his back, his eyes wild as he stared up at Sam.

"You're skilled at lying, ain't cha?" Sam growled out. "She wasn't here at all, was she? What's your game, Mormon? Are you really ready to die?"

"No, please don't kill me," Jeremiah begged. "She must have fled in the night. I guess she didn't like what I offered her here at our community . . . a safe haven!"

"If she was here at all, I'd say it was probably you that she fled from," Sam said, laughing mockingly. "What'd you do? Tell her that she was going to make one of your men another wife? Or . . . did you tell her that you wanted her all to yoreself?"

Jeremiah struggled to understand how Nicole could have left. There were sentries standing guard everywhere.

Surely someone had seen her leave . . . and allowed it. But if all the sentries had been killed, he might never know.

Sam shrugged. "Well, okay, she's gone," he said, walking past Jeremiah. He stopped before leaving the house. "But she can't be far away if she left this place during the night. Mark my word, Mormon, I'll find 'er."

Sam laughed sardonically. "Do you know, I'm not sure which punishment would be worse for her?" he said. "Bringin' her back here to live with the likes of you and your people, or takin' her for myself to do with as I wish."

Again Sam shrugged and left, leaving Jeremiah gasping on the floor, stunned that he had been allowed to live. He lay there until he heard the horses ride away.

He waited a while longer before he got up. Then he scrambled to his feet and ran outside, where everyone who had been in the dining hall was now gathered. The two wives of the fallen man were kneeling over him, along with his three children. All were weeping.

It was apparent that everyone was in a state of shock. They all looked to Jeremiah for answers.

Jeremiah went to them and stood before them. "Seems we had quite a problem on our hands, but I've taken care of it," he said thickly. "Those men came to Hope looking for Nicole. Well, they came too late, for she left our community during the night. Seems she wasn't satisfied with the haven we offered her here and she managed to talk one of our own into allowing her to leave."

He hung his head. "We'll never know which man allowed this, for without even going to look, I feel sure all of those who stood sentry last night were killed by the murdering outlaws," he said sadly. He looked up at his people. "I'm sorry, so sorry. You know that I didn't ask for any of this to happen, but I do feel responsible since I was the one who insisted on bringing Nicole among us."

He looked at the children, whose eyes were filled with tears. He looked at the men who now stood together, their wives huddling as they held their children closer.

"Go and find those who were victims of the madmen," Jeremiah said. "Perhaps one among them might still be alive."

His head hanging, Jeremiah walked away from them all. He went to his home and locked himself into his room.

He had been so wrong to bring Nicole back to Hope. That woman had brought death with her.

It seemed to follow wherever she went.

Feeling so responsible for the tragedy that had come to Hope, Jeremiah bowed his head in shame.

Chapter Twenty-six

In the air there was the aroma of food cooking, alerting Nicole that they must be nearing Eagle Wolf's stronghold.

A moment later, Eagle Wolf led her through a small pass, and Nicole got her first glimpse of the tops of tepees with smoke wafting in soft, gray spirals from their smoke holes.

As she rode with Eagle Wolf just a bit farther down the narrow path, she saw the entire village lying nestled in a hidden valley. The sight of a waterfall at the far side, cascading beautifully from a tall cliff, drew Nicole's breath away. She had never seen anything as grand and majestic as that water falling in such a long stream, down, down, into a beautiful river that ran along one side of the village.

Nicole saw some women at the river, bending over the water, filling jugs with it. Others walked leisurely away from the river, each carrying a jug on her shoulder.

Farther still, to her left, she saw a huge garden, where women were busy harvesting what Nicole recognized as corn, beans, and beautiful, golden squash, as well as other vegetables. It was obvious that these people needed no one else for their survival.

Nicole also saw sheep in pens, their wool thick and ready to be shorn to make warm clothes for the winter. Then she wondered, would she be spending the winter here among the Navaho?

She was a woman with white skin. Surely she would be seen as these peoples' enemy, for was it not people with white skin who had forced them into hiding?

The thought of their not accepting her caused a sick feeling in the pit of Nicole's stomach. If they didn't, what then would Eagle Wolf do about her?

Would he put her above everyone else and allow her to stay among his people? Or would he do their bidding if they told him that they did not want her to stay among them?

Oh, Lord, would he turn her away so that she was all alone in the world once again?

Oh, surely not.

At that moment, Eagle Wolf reached over and grabbed her reins to stop her horse, drawing his own to a stop beside her.

She looked into his eyes, seeing an emotion in them that told her of the depths of his love for her.

She didn't know how this love had happened since they were of two different worlds.

And it had happened so quickly.

But they did love each other!

"You must know that you are not only a stranger to my people, but someone who looks like their most hated enemy," Eagle Wolf said thickly. "I am not certain how my Owl Clan will react when they see you with me. But I am confident that when they know you as I do, they will no longer see you as an enemy, but someone welcome in their lives."

"I'm so nervous," Nicole murmured. "What will you do if they refuse to accept me? Will . . . you . . . send me away?"

"You know that I could never do that," Eagle Wolf said. He reached over with his free hand and gently took one of hers. "The moment we met, I knew it was our destiny to become one. You felt it, too. I know, because I see that truth in your eyes every time you look into mine. My Great Spirit will guide my people into accepting, and then, loving you."

"But I am being thrust into their lives so suddenly, without any warning," Nicole said, her voice breaking.

"Not altogether," Eagle Wolf said, slowly taking his hand from hers. "I was not alone when I first saw you at the Mormon community. Several of my warriors rode with me. When they returned to our home without me, I have no doubt they told our people about you. They knew that I would be bringing you home with me."

"I feel uncomfortable because I know how often the Indians have been tricked by my people's government," Nicole said softly. "I know about broken treaties."

"Yes, my Navaho tribe is one of those that were tricked more than once because we trusted too easily," Eagle Wolf said tightly. "That is why I have brought my Owl Clan into hiding. There are no boundaries here as there are on reservations where the white people have forced so many red-skinned people to go. We have made our own boundaries. We are happy here."

"But don't you see, Eagle Wolf?" Nicole murmured. "I might be too much of a reminder of all that for your people to accept me."

"In time you will prove to them that you are a different sort of person," Eagle Wolf said, in his eyes a determination to make her understand that she need not be afraid to venture onward into his village. "So come now, Nicole. Come and let me show you to my people. There will be some who will be hard to convince that you are a person whose heart is good. But in time, those people will see you as I do."

"But you are . . ." Nicole broke off, blushing because she had almost said that he was in love with her.

"I know what you were going to say without your saying it," Eagle Wolf said, smiling softly at her. "I see it in the sudden change of color on your face."

He again reached over and took one of her hands in his. "*Ho*, I am in love with you, and, yes, love sometimes clouds one's reasoning. But know this, woman, I can be in love, and make sense, too," he said, chuckling.

"How could you know what I did not say?" Nicole asked, in awe of this man's sensitivity.

"Your feelings are in your eyes," Eagle Wolf said, bringing her hand to his lips and gently kissing it. "You love me. I love you. Now it is said aloud. My warriors have told my people how I feel about you. They will make you welcome at our village in all ways."

Loving this man so much, Nicole wanted to be kissed by him, and not only on the hand.

As though Eagle Wolf had once again read her thoughts, he reached for her. Leaning closer, he soon had her in his arms, his lips warm and wonderful on hers.

She twined her arms around his neck.

The moment was magical and wonderful as she tasted the wonder of his lips and felt the strength in his arms as he kept her from falling off her horse, while she was leaning toward him.

She knew that life was going to be all right for her again, and all because of this man who had welcomed her into his heart against all odds.

"I love you," he whispered against her lips. "*Ka-bike-hozhoni-bi*, forever, my woman. Forever. Now let me take you to my people and let them love you, too."

Nicole's heart was hammering inside her chest as he drew away from her and gave her her reins.

"This is our time. Let us go onward into a world that now belongs to both of us," Eagle Wolf said. He smiled at her. "*Daltso-hozhoni*. All is beautiful."

He looked straight ahead again, then sank his moccasined heels into the flanks of his white steed.

Nicole rode with him into the outer fringes of the village.

Everyone stopped what they were doing when they saw the white woman with their chief. All of Nicole's fears returned in one leap of a heartbeat as she saw resentment on many of the peoples' faces.

Yet on the children's faces was no resentment. Sweet and innocent, they clung to the skirts of their mother's buckskin dresses, gazing up at Nicole with wide, brown eyes.

Some children even smiled, although bashfully, as Nicole rode past them. It was then she knew that things would be all right.

She thought about how these children had been cheated of so many things because of what white people had done to them. She felt ashamed at first, and then she found herself loving the children.

She envisioned herself standing before a group of these children, whose trusting eyes watched her as she taught them everything she could.

Yes! These Navaho children would be her students.

As they rode onward, Eagle Wolf smiled from one person to the other, nodding his head at those who openly greeted him, and Nicole began to feel less and less uncomfortable. She could almost see people beginning to relax toward her.

And then someone suddenly stepped away from the others, blocking Eagle Wolf and Nicole's way.

They were forced to come to an abrupt halt, stopping only a few inches from the angry-eyed man who faced them with fists jammed angrily on his hips.

He wore only a breechclout and moccasins. His coal-black hair fell in a long braid down his back. A knife was sheathed at his right side, glinting threateningly as the sun played on its handle.

Nicole realized that she had just found her first Navaho enemy, and she could not help being afraid.

Where there was one, surely there were others.

She glanced quickly at Eagle Wolf, who stayed in his saddle even as his eyes battled with those of the warrior. The other man stood there, glaring directly into Eagle Wolf's eyes.

This warrior was openly challenging his chief. Nicole was stunned to witness this exchange.

"My brother, step aside," Eagle Wolf said tightly. "You do not know what you are doing."

"I know very well, my brother," Spirit Wolf said. He slowly shifted his glare over to Nicole, making her shudder at the coldness in his eyes.

Nicole knew now that this was Eagle Wolf's blood kin . . . his brother, and she could tell there was no love lost between them.

Nicole waited to see how Eagle Wolf would react to this brother who seemed so out of line and perhaps an embarrassment to Eagle Wolf.

"Spirit Wolf, step aside," Eagle Wolf said again, this time with more anger and strength behind his words.

"Eagle Wolf, my brother and chief, you are not acting wisely, bringing this woman into our lives," Spirit Wolf said. "Are you blind, brother? Do you not see the color of her skin? She is white! One white among us will bring more. Surely someone will want to know where she is. They will come here. Our stronghold will no longer be safe because of this one white woman!"

Eagle Wolf dismounted.

He went to Spirit Wolf and stood directly before him, but he did not reach out and touch him . . . yet.

Eagle Wolf was a man of self-control, and at this moment, he needed all that he could gather within himself to deal with his brother's disobedience.

"And so my brother shames his own brother . . . his chief . . . in the presence of others?" Eagle Wolf said coolly. "You know well, Spirit Wolf, that I would never bring harm to our people. This woman will not bring harm, either. She is kind. And she is alone. This woman lost her family. She is alone in this world. Only the Mormon people know that she survived the wrath of those who killed her parents, and those Mormons would not dare come on our mountain. She is not of their religion, or their kind. And they are not the sort of people who cause trouble. They follow their own rules of goodness and kindness, leaving others alone."

He turned and looked at his people. "Know this, my people," he said, gazing from one to the other. "All is safe at our stronghold. This woman, too, seeks safety from those who killed her parents. She has suffered terrible losses. She deserves peace in her life. Like you, she deserves a safe haven. I have offered this to her, and she has accepted."

Spirit Wolf stepped even closer to Eagle Wolf, so close that their breaths mixed.

"How do you know this white woman so well? Why would you do this for her?" Spirit Wolf asked, his eyes mocking.

"This woman came to me when I was sick with fever. She offered me help while you, my very own brother, were trying to benefit from your brother's illness," Eagle Wolf said dryly. "If I must choose between the two of you, I prefer to have her in my life."

Eagle Wolf stepped away from Spirit Wolf and pointed to the path that led down the mountain. "Go, Spirit Wolf," he said, his voice filled with deep emotion. "You do not deserve the love or loyalty of your chieftain brother, or our people. In your heart there lies too much envy toward your own blood brother, your only family left on this earth. You have lost the right to my love. Our parents would be ashamed of you, as ashamed as I am."

Shocked by Eagle Wolf's sudden decision to send him out of his life, Spirit Wolf stepped away from his brother, wide-eyed. "You would do this to your brother?" he gasped. "You would send me away?"

"You sent yourself away when you decided to become someone I no longer recognize," Eagle Wolf said. "All of our lives I have cared for you, my brother. And still you resent me and my position in life? Spirit Wolf, go away and think about what you have done and what you have wanted to do to your brother. When, and if, you can return and be the person you were before greed and jealousy came into your heart, you will be welcome again in our Owl Clan."

"You would do this because . . . because . . . of this woman?" Spirit Wolf blurted out, again glaring at Nicole. "It is because of her and you know it!"

"You are still not listening to my words or my heart, brother," Eagle Wolf said. He pointed toward the pass that led from the village. "Go. Now."

Suddenly realizing that Eagle Wolf was serious, and that he was near to being banished from their clan, Spirit Wolf grew downcast. "I am sorry," he cried. "I spoke out of turn. Please forgive me. Give me a second chance. I do love you, Eagle Wolf. Greed and the desire for leadership did blind me, but only for a little while. I no longer want what my brother rightfully has. Please forgive me?"

Nicole felt partly to blame for what had just happened between the two brothers. She wanted to try to do something to smooth things over between them.

She dismounted and went to Eagle Wolf, placing a soft hand on his arm. Eagle Wolf looked at her with a question in his eyes.

"Eagle Wolf, a person is much bigger and better if he can find it in his heart to forgive, especially family," she murmured. "Spirit Wolf is your brother. Please give him a second chance. I know how quickly one can lose family, for always. You, too, could lose your brother in such a way."

Both Eagle Wolf and Spirit Wolf gazed in wonder at her. Both saw the goodness of her heart.

Of course, Eagle Wolf had already seen it, but this new evidence of it confirmed how right he was to have brought her to his stronghold.

Eagle Wolf nodded. He truly did not want to lose his brother. Spirit Wolf was all that was left of their family.

It would devastate him if he could never see Spirit Wolf again.

He reached out and embraced his brother, holding him tightly. "We must never let anything pull us apart again," he said thickly. "Our mother and father would not rest in the heavens if we were not good to each other. My brother, do not leave. Stay. We will work things out between us."

Spirit Wolf choked back a sob and clung to Eagle Wolf.

In Navaho, he told him that he was sorry.

"Truly, my brother, I will never disappoint you again," Spirit Wolf then said. "*Ukehe*, thank you."

They stepped apart.

They both turned to Nicole and smiled at her.

Through all of this, the people of the Owl Clan were silent, looking and listening. Now they were smiling.

Suddenly the onlookers went to Nicole. One by one, they embraced her and welcomed her.

She realized now that by acting to bring the brothers together again, she had made the people see that she was no danger to them.

They were openly letting Eagle Wolf know, without words, that this woman needed protection from the outside world, and they were willing to provide it.

Eagle Wolf nodded to two youths. They came to him and took the horses.

Eagle Wolf took Nicole by the hand and led her to his tepee. When he had the entrance flap closed, he turned and pulled her into his arms.

She twined her arms around his neck and melted as his lips came to hers in a wondrous kiss.

Then she leaned away from him and smiled into his eyes. "Thank you," she murmured.

"And why do you thank me?" Eagle Wolf asked, his eyes dancing.

"For being you," she murmured. "Just for . . . being . . . you."

Again he swept her against him and kissed her. The world went on outside the lodge, laughter and voices and sunshine wafting down through the smoke hole overhead.

Suddenly Nicole believed in life again. For a while she had given up hoping that it would ever be worth living again.

Now she had a reason. She had many.

There was Eagle Wolf. There were the Navaho children.

Ah, but she was anxious to see their eyes as she stood before them, teaching them to read and write, and to understand the ways of white people.

This band of Navaho would not be tricked again by false treaties, that was for certain.

She would make it so.

Chapter Twenty-seven

Tired from the long climb on horseback to Eagle Wolf's stronghold, Nicole was glad to finally be inside the tepee with his arms so warm and wonderful around her.

And the kiss!

She never would have imagined a kiss could stir so many feelings within a woman as his kiss had caused inside her.

Eagle Wolf was still holding her hand as they both turned to go and sit beside a fire that someone had kept burning for Eagle Wolf while he was gone.

Having never been in a tepee before, Nicole marveled at what she saw.

She could tell that the tepee was new. She not only could see the newness, she could smell it. It was a nice, clean smell.

She looked slowly around her at what the tepee held. It was like nothing she had ever seen before. The entire floor of the tepee was covered with colorful bulrush mats, and there were brightly colored blankets rolled up and placed along one wall.

It was a warm, comfortable place, and larger than she'd thought a tepee could be. There was certainly room for a family of Navaho to eat and sleep comfortably.

"And now you see how this chief lives," Eagle Wolf said, noting how she had taken everything in as she looked slowly around her. "It is not like what you are used to. Will you be comfortable enough?"

Nicole looked quickly at him, blushing. "I am to stay here with you?" she asked, surprised. Then she tried not to act as though she was bothered by the idea, for she truly could not see herself living anywhere else now that they had declared their love for each other.

She was learning about life and how quickly a person's circumstances could change. Before all of these changes came into her life, she took each day without much thought of tomorrow.

While growing up, she never had reason to fear the future. She had been happy. Her mother had doted on her, and for a long time she had not known about her father's gambling.

So why would she have a reason to wonder if tomorrow would even come? She always knew that it would.

But now?

Her world had changed.

Nothing was the same as it had been before she'd arrived at Tyler City and seen what hate could do to one's life. It had been Sam Partain's hate that had changed everything for Nicole.

But one of those changes had been a good one, for she was with the most wonderful man in the world. Eagle Wolf had brought sunshine back into her life.

He gave her a reason to want to wake up each morning, for she would awaken now, knowing that he would be there for her. He would protect her.

Eagle Wolf was taken aback by Nicole's question about her staying with him in his lodge.

He had never thought that might be a problem. They had confessed their love for each other, and he had assumed a wedding ceremony would come soon after.

But now? He wondered whether she wanted the same.

"I am certain that all the sudden changes in your life have been difficult for you," Eagle Wolf said as he reached over and took one of her hands in his. "I want to change your life back to something wonderful and good. If you are uncomfortable about sharing a lodge with me, I will understand."

He gazed into her eyes and was glad when he did not see anything now but love and peace in their depths.

"I do not want you to think that I was bothered by what you said," Nicole murmured. She reached up and covered his hand, feeling truly blessed to have met such a man, one who would look out for her best interests, and who loved her.

"I would love to share this tepee with you," Nicole murmured. "Eagle Wolf, I adore it . . . I adore you."

"My love for you is strong," Eagle Wolf said thickly. "I realize that we have not known each other for long, but love sometimes comes quickly, as it has for us. When it does, one must grasp what is offered from above and protect it. I will protect you and my feelings for you, forever."

"As I will you," Nicole murmured.

Her pulse was racing, for she knew that she was moments away from being kissed once again by this man who stirred sensual feelings she had not known existed within her.

No, she had not known passion, not until she gazed into his eyes that first time and saw, even though he was gripped by fever, that he was a man among men.

She had been born to love him.

Eagle Wolf leaned over and slid his arms around Nicole's waist, drawing her close to him.

His lips were only an inch from hers when a voice spoke from behind the closed entrance flap.

"My brother, I have brought Dancing Snow Feather with me so that she can know Nicole," Spirit Wolf said.

"I have brought food," Dancing Snow Feather

added, her voice wafting through the entrance flap, sounding to Nicole like a soft, sweet song.

Nicole had not yet seen the woman, but from the sound of her voice, she expected Dancing Snow Feather to be beautiful and sweet.

Nicole and Eagle Wolf quickly parted and rose to their feet.

Nicole stood back from the fire as Eagle Wolf went to draw open the entrance flap, stepping aside so that Spirit Wolf and his wife could enter the tepee.

He was happy that his brother had come to him with his wife, for it proved that Spirit Wolf was again his brother in every way.

Spirit Wolf had always been a kind and caring man. It just seemed that for a while he had lost his way.

He was back again, the brother whom Eagle Wolf had always loved and protected.

Nicole was instantly taken by the pretty young woman who entered the tepee ahead of Spirit Wolf. In her hands was a wooden tray with many delicious-looking offerings of food spread across it.

In one glance, Nicole saw meat, corn on the cob, and other vegetables. She also saw a freshly sliced apple. Apparently, not only vegetables were grown at this stronghold; there must also be apple trees somewhere close by.

Spirit Wolf stepped quickly to Dancing Snow

Feather's side and took the tray from her. He set it down on the floor beside the fire.

All the while, Nicole was still gazing at the lovely, tiny woman, whose snow-white dress, surely of doeskin, contrasted with her copper skin.

Dancing Snow Feather's black hair hung in one long braid down her back, with beads woven into the strands.

Nicole then noticed that a soft red color had been painted in the part of Dancing Snow Feather's hair. There was also a touch of red on her cheeks.

All in all, she was breathtakingly beautiful. Nicole was glad that she was someone else's wife, or she would be afraid of losing the man she loved to this woman.

"Nicole, I am Dancing Snow Feather," the young woman said in a voice as lovely as herself. "I have brought you food. It is my way to welcome you among us."

"Thank you," Nicole murmured. "I truly appreciate it."

She eyed the food on the tray again. She had not realized that she was so hungry. But now the sight of the food made her stomach growl, drawing a giggle from Dancing Snow Feather.

"My brother, you and your woman are welcome in my lodge," Eagle Wolf said, embracing Spirit Wolf with a manly hug.

He gently embraced Dancing Snow Feather. "*Ukehe*. Thank you for the food," he said. "It is good of you to share with your chief and the woman who now joins our people."

"My chief, you were gone for so long, I was sure you would be hungry," Dancing Snow Feather said softly, returning Eagle Wolf's embrace. "The gift of food is for you both from both of us."

Eagle Wolf stepped away from her and went to the back of the tepee, where he grabbed up a blanket.

He took it back to where everyone still stood and shook the blanket out, then spread it beside the fire.

With a hand he gestured toward it. "Sit with us and share the food," he invited, looking from Dancing Snow Feather to his brother.

When Dancing Snow Feather gave Nicole a questioning look, as if to ask her permission, Nicole smiled at her. "Please stay," she murmured. "And thank you so much for thinking of us. It has been a while since we ate."

It seemed so strange to Nicole, yet wonderful, to say "we" when referring to herself and Eagle Wolf. It felt as though they were already married and accepting company into their lodge.

Dancing Snow Feather smiled broadly as she sat down. Nicole sat beside her, while the brothers seated themselves beside each other.

"I did not prepare all of the food by myself," Dancing Snow Feather admitted reluctantly. She had seen the admiration in Nicole's eyes and realized that the white woman thought Dancing Snow Feather had cooked everything on the tray.

She hated for Nicole to know that she was not all that skilled with food preparation. She seemed so clumsy. Soiled spots on many of the bulrush mats in her lodge proved it. She was always spilling something or other.

This clumsiness embarrassed her and she was glad that her husband had accepted her failings.

Dancing Snow Feather pointed to the meat. "My friend Tiny Fawn prepared the mutton," she murmured. "Another friend made this corn."

Nicole accepted a delicious-looking piece of corn on the cob. She passed the tray on, and soon they all had chosen what they wanted and were eating and talking and smiling.

Nicole felt quite comfortable with everyone and hoped this was something that they would do often. She felt at ease with Eagle Wolf's brother and wife. In fact, she looked forward to having the beautiful Navaho woman as a good friend.

After all the food was gone, and Nicole was caught yawning by Eagle Wolf, he stood up, reached for the empty wooden tray, and handed it to Dancing Snow Feather.

"It was good sharing with you and my brother," he said, smiling into her eyes. "We shall do this often."

Dancing Snow Feather beamed at the suggestion. She glanced up at Eagle Wolf, then smiled at Nicole as she rose to stand beside Eagle Wolf.

The two brothers embraced; then soon Eagle Wolf and Nicole were alone. He caught her yawning again and rubbing her eyes.

He turned to her and drew her into a gentle embrace. "It is time now for you to sleep," he murmured. "It has been a long day."

Nicole could not help it. She yawned again, then laughed softly as she gazed into Eagle Wolf's dark eyes. "I guess I do need a wink or two," she said, noticing a look of confusion on his face.

She realized that he did not understand what she meant.

"When I say a wink or two, it means a little bit of sleep," she murmured, loving the fact that she could make him smile as he was smiling at her now.

"You shall have as much sleep as you need, and then tomorrow I will take you all around our stronghold and introduce you to each of my people. I will show you our animals, as well as our garden, which fed us tonight. I think I can already guess your favorite vegetable . . . corn on the cob," he said softly.

"Yes, I guess I did make a pig of myself eating more than one piece of corn," Nicole murmured, then realized that she had said something else that puzzled him.

She immediately knew what it had been. She had said that she'd made a pig of herself, an expression her father had always used after eating too much of his wife's cooking.

She explained this phrase to Eagle Wolf, too, and they laughed together as they went to the pile of blankets and each chose one to sleep on for the night.

After the blanket was spread for Nicole, she enjoyed one more embrace from Eagle Wolf, then stretched out beside the fire while he made his bed on the other side.

Nicole was soon asleep, yet Eagle Wolf found himself unable to close his eyes so quickly. He could not take his eyes off this woman who he knew would soon be his wife.

He could not believe that he had found a woman to love. Not only someone to bear him children, but to truly have and hold and love.

Ho, his feelings for this woman were very different from those he'd felt for his departed wife. Theirs had been a marriage of convenience, with much admiration for each other, but not the strong love he felt for Nicole.

Since he was chief, he knew the importance of having sons, and so he had married. But his wife had been taken from him before she could have even one child.

Eagle Wolf knew that Nicole would be the mother of his children. Even better, she would bring joy to his heart because of the deep love they shared for each other.

He smiled and stretched out on his back, watching the stars blinking back at him through the smoke hole overhead.

"*Daltso-hozhoni. Ho, daltso-hozhoni*, all is beautiful in the world now that I have found the woman who was sent to me from the Great Spirit above," he whispered to himself.

Chapter Twenty-eight

Nicole was so glad to have finally gotten a good night's rest, in a place where she felt safe, and loved.

It was early morning now and she had been given a basin of water for bathing. While she had washed herself, Eagle Wolf had gone down to the river where he had bathed with several of his warriors, and talked over the upcoming day's activities.

But Eagle Wolf had returned now to his tepee, his long, black hair sleekly wet down his bare copper back. All that he had on was a breechclout that covered only what was necessary for modesty's sake.

As Nicole sat there before the lodge fire, she felt especially pretty today. She was wearing one of several dresses that had been brought to Eagle Wolf's lodge by the women of the village. They were gifts for the newcomer.

Today's was a soft, white doeskin, embellished with various shells and beads along the hem of the skirt.

The neckline swept down low, leaving Nicole a

little self-conscious because the upper swells of her breasts were exposed.

As Eagle Wolf stood across the fire from where she sat, using a cloth to dry his long, black hair, Nicole caught his occasional admiring glance at that part of her body she rarely had shown to anyone.

She self-consciously swept a hand up over her breasts, eliciting a soft chuckle from Eagle Wolf as he caught her blushing.

"My woman, if you knew just how beautiful you look sitting there beside my lodge fire, with the glow of the fire on not only your cheeks, but also your breasts, you would not think to cover any of it from the view of this man who loves you," Eagle Wolf said, glad when his words brought a smile to her face.

"I do find the dress so pretty," Nicole said as she slowly moved her hand from her breasts. "And it is so soft. That was what I was doing. I was feeling the softness of the dress."

She smiled and shook her head, knowing she wasn't being completely honest.

"Oh, well, yes, I must admit that I was feeling a bit shy a moment ago," she said, now laughing softly as she gazed into his dark eyes.

"And now?" he asked, tossing the cloth aside. "You are no longer shy? You are comfortable?"

"Yes, very," Nicole said, again smiling. "And it is so generous of the women of your village to give me these beautiful dresses."

She gazed down at the beads and shells on the skirt of the dress. She ran a hand slowly over them. "The shells and beads are so beautiful and delicate," she murmured, then gazed up at him. "I love them. I love everything about all of the dresses."

"You look beautiful in them," Eagle Wolf said, then went and knelt beside her, his back to her. "Would you braid my hair for me?"

Surprised by his request, yet glad to have the opportunity to touch his beautiful hair, and to be so near him, Nicole nodded. "I would love to," she murmured.

Then she said something that seemed to come from nowhere. "Will you braid mine after I finish yours?" she blurted out.

She had never worn her hair in braids. But now it seemed the natural thing to do after seeing so many of the Navaho women with braids.

"I can do yours first," Eagle Wolf said, glancing at her over his shoulder.

"No, I want to do yours first," Nicole murmured, already separating his hair so that she could braid it. "I have noticed that several warriors wear their hair in one braid, yet I have seen some wear two. Which do you prefer?"

"You braid it as you would wish to see it," Eagle Wolf said, feeling more and more attached to this woman. They were united in every way a man and woman could be.

Except for making love. He would not initiate that until he knew she was absolutely ready.

He didn't need to ask whether or not she was a virgin. He knew this already. She was not the sort of woman to give herself to a man until wedding vows would soon be spoken between her and the man she chose to love.

"One long braid fascinates me," Nicole murmured.

"That is my favorite, too, so braid mine that way and then I will braid yours," Eagle Wolf said, feeling her tugging on his hair as she carefully made each twist and turn.

"It has just begun to rain," Nicole murmured, hearing the drops fall softly against the outside buckskin of the tepee. "I love softly falling rain. Do you?"

"Yes, I always have," Eagle Wolf said, gazing upward through the smoke hole. The sky was not very dark, so he thought that this might be a brief rain.

He could smell its sweetness.

He recalled as a child how he'd enjoyed this sort of rain. He would run through it with his friends, splashing their bare feet in the puddles. They would play outside until all the mothers made their children come inside their lodges. This would happen instantly if a clap of thunder reminded them that there could be danger from lightning.

He and his friends would then scatter in all directions until they had gotten safely into their lodges with their mothers and fathers.

Eagle Wolf had always been especially proud to be with his parents, for his father was the chief of their people, a proud, stately man, the kind of leader Eagle Wolf aspired to be.

His mother had always been just as special to him, but in different ways. No one could have been as sweet and caring as his mother.

He could even now remember the warmth of her arms as she would embrace and comfort him when an extra-loud crash of thunder shook the floor of their tepee.

Today there was no lightning or thunder, only the continuing soft pitter-patter of the raindrops against the sides of the lodge.

"There are rains of two types," Eagle Wolf said as Nicole continued braiding his hair.

"Soft and hard," Nicole responded, laughingly. She knew this was not what he was about to say, but it felt good to be lighthearted and gay with him.

Eagle Wolf laughed. He was glad she could be so lighthearted after the sorrow these past days had brought into her life. Some people who experienced the same might never smile or laugh again.

But this woman was the sort who would never allow anything to take away her joy in living. She loved life as much as he.

And that, too, brought them closer together. In so many ways they were so much alike.

They would be happy as husband and wife, and

they would marvel at the children they'd bring together into this world.

"There is female rain and there is male rain," Eagle Wolf said.

His comment was so unexpected, Nicole stopped braiding his hair for a moment, so that she could move around to gaze into his eyes.

"Female and male?" she asked. "How can there be . . . female and male rain?"

"This was taught me as a child by my mother," Eagle Wolf said as Nicole returned to braiding his long hair. "She taught me that the soaking, yet soft rain is called female, because it is the rain that nurtures and nourishes. Not only plants, but also animals, as it settles gently upon them from the heavens."

"Why, that is beautiful," Nicole murmured, then went around and sat beside Eagle Wolf after securing his long braid with a short piece of leather thong.

"What is the male rain responsible for?" she asked.

"Male rain is not gentle in any respect," Eagle Wolf said, reaching back and touching his braid, smiling his approval of how perfectly it had been formed.

"No?" Nicole said as he brought his hand away from his braid and reached over to grab a stick and slowly stir the ashes in the fire, causing sparks to fly upward through the smoke hole overhead.

"As most men are seen by women, the male rain is powerful," Eagle Wolf said.

He dropped the glowing, fiery stick, then settled back from the fire, now gazing into Nicole's grass green eyes.

"This is the destructive rain of the most vicious storms," he said. "Ofttimes trees are destroyed during these storms, not nourished. Animals run and hide, as do women and children. But strong warriors never run from such rain. Instead, it rekindles their own inner fires, and makes them the sort of warriors who keep our people safe from harm."

Suddenly, out of nowhere, blinding light from a streak of lightning flashed downward through the smoke hole.

The suddenness of it, the brightness, caused Nicole to flinch. When the ensuing thunder rocked the floor on which she was sitting, she flung herself into Eagle Wolf's arms and clung to him.

He wrapped his arms around her and held her close. He could feel the rapidness of her breathing against his bare chest.

"I have always been afraid of storms," Nicole said, realizing that she was trembling in his arms, and feeling embarrassed over it.

But nothing had ever been able to take the fear of storms away from her. When she had been a small child, a horrible tornado had torn through Missouri, destroying most of the homes close to Nicole's.

It had uprooted some of the largest elm trees in the area. Some homes had caught fire from the lightning strikes. Some people's lives were lost.

Her family had been fortunate not to have lost anything except for a few horses that had broken through their corral fence and run off.

"You are safe with me," Eagle Wolf softly reassured her as he slowly caressed her back through the softness of her dress. "I will never allow anything or anyone to harm you. Nor will the Great Spirit. He sees everything and knows what you have been forced to endure. You will be always safe while you are with me."

"I do feel so safe, yet the lightning and thunder always frighten me," Nicole murmured, still clinging, even though she was no longer really afraid. She did believe that Eagle Wolf and his Great Spirit, as well as her own God, would keep her safe.

"When I was a child, lightning struck many things and set them afire," Nicole murmured. "My neighbor's house went up in flames during one of our worst storms. And then there were the tornadoes that we had to endure more than once. Some even called our portion of Missouri 'tornado alley.'"

"I am not familiar with tornadoes," Eagle Wolf said, releasing her as she nudged herself away from him.

"It is a horrific sort of wind," Nicole murmured, visibly trembling at the remembrance. "It just seems to fall down from the darkened sky, swirling and swirling, taking everything in its path. I grew to dread them so much. I hope I never see any again."

"We have no such winds on our mountain, yet we do have winds that sometimes bend the corn in half so that the tassels touch the ground," Eagle Wolf said somberly. "I will protect you from those winds and anything else that threatens you. Know this, Nicole. You are safe with me."

He took her hands in his. "Our shaman has been known to speak and stop the winds," he said softly. "Our shaman understands power and how to control it, even the power of lightning. You see, objects struck by lightning hold within them the power of holy beings. A shaman can use this kind of power to heal, or to bring sickness to an enemy."

"Are you saying that lightning-struck objects can be used for both good and bad?" Nicole asked.

"*Ho,*" Eagle Wolf said, nodding. "Lightning is used both for protection and healing, as well as to cause death and destruction."

"I have always been afraid of lightning and now I will be even more afraid of it," Nicole said, again shuddering.

"I did not tell you these things to frighten you, but to teach you things my people know," Eagle Wolf said, thickly. "Sometimes learning can be fearful, but only if those who are taught these things allow it to be. You are with me. You have no need to fear any of these things."

"You are right," Nicole said, smiling at him. "If I ever doubt that again, I will remind myself what you have said to me, more than once. I truly feel safe, Eagle Wolf, now that I am with you."

Eagle Wolf placed his hands on her cheeks and drew her close to him, until their lips were barely an inch apart. And then he swept his fingers behind her, twining them through her hair, which he had not yet braided.

He brought her lips to his and gave her a kiss that was so hot she felt as though she might melt through the bulrush mats beneath her.

She had never known what true desire was until she had met Eagle Wolf. Now she knew how it felt to want someone so badly she ached from it. She felt a hunger she had never experienced before. Her body, heart, and soul were crying out to make love with this wonderful man.

But she could not be brazen enough to initiate such a thing. She did not want to remember their first lovemaking in such a way.

Yet she did ache for him, oh, so badly.

Eagle Wolf's body ached more than he had ever felt before. His need for Nicole at this moment was almost unbearable.

He kissed her with a passion that had only now been unleashed within him. These feelings were far more intense than he had ever felt for the woman he had made his wife.

This woman in his arms was meant to be there. They had been destined to meet.

And they were destined to marry and have children.

But he did not want to rush her into lovemaking. He did not want her to think that was the only reason he'd rescued her.

He knew how she had felt about the Mormon and his impure intentions. Eagle Wolf desired her, too, but he wanted her for herself. And he wanted her forever.

Perhaps tomorrow they could make love. But not today, nor tonight.

"I will love you always," he whispered against her hot lips.

"I love you, too," Nicole whispered back to him. "I have never felt like this. I . . . I . . . feel as though I am flying above myself. Everything in me feels light and wonderful."

"We are flying together," Eagle Wolf replied. He held her away from him so that they could look into each other's eyes. "I want you, Nicole. All of you. But I don't think it is right yet to blend our hearts and souls in the way my body is aching to do. I want you to have more time to think and be sure. So much has happened in your life. I want you to know your heart and mind completely, to be sure you wish to accept what I am offering you. I want you to marry me. Will you be my wife?"

Nicole was thrilled that this man truly loved her enough to marry her.

Promises of protection were one thing. But a promise of marriage was the ultimate commitment.

"Yes, oh, yes," she murmured. She flung herself into his arms.

He wanted to postpone what their bodies ached for, and she knew that was right, so she just hugged him and his words to her heart.

This moment would always be precious to her, for it was the moment they gave their hearts to each other.

For Nicole the future was once again promising and wonderful. Because of Eagle Wolf.

"It is my turn now to braid your hair," he said, gently holding her away from him. Then he turned her so that her back was to him. He lifted her hair, sniffed its clean smell, then began braiding it, slowly, almost meditatively, for this moment was one he would never forget.

It marked the beginning of their lives together.

Chapter Twenty-nine

It was midmorning as Nicole rode her mare beside Eagle Wolf's majestic white stallion.

While they had eaten the breakfast that Dancing Snow Feather had brought to them, Eagle Wolf had said that he wanted to acquaint Nicole with this wondrous land that was now her home.

They had been riding for perhaps an hour beneath the cottonwoods, their yellow leaves brilliant in the morning sun.

The grass that had been so green and bright only a few weeks ago was now turning brown and blew stiffly in the wind today. Only a few wildflowers remained, their colors now faded and their stems wilted from last night's sudden frost.

Nicole could hear the splash of the waterfall, and she marveled at the rainbows formed as the water plummeted to the river below.

She glanced over at Eagle Wolf, feeling the connection between them, which she still marveled over. The soft breeze on the mountain lifted his long and flowing hair so that it blew behind him like sleek, black satin.

She was glad that he had chosen to leave his hair loose today. She loved to see it and run her fingers through it.

She loved to smell it, too. It always smelled clean, like fresh river water!

Today he wore only a breechclout, and most of his copper body was revealed to Nicole. She marveled over his muscles and his handsomeness as though this were the first time she had seen him.

It was not only his looks that had captured her heart. She would never stop appreciating his kindness toward her.

It seemed a miracle that she had been led to him that day, where he lay so ill beneath a tree. Had she chosen a different path up the mountain, she would never have seen him or known the love of this man who had given his all to her.

Soon they would be married.

He had told her that he must go on a hunt before they could stand together and speak the words that would make them husband and wife. The autumn hunt. He would leave tomorrow.

But today was theirs, and he rode beside her to acquaint her with his land, the marvels of it.

She was glad that the breeze had turned warm. When they first arose this morning and stepped outside for a breath of fresh air, frost had lain on the pumpkins that had not yet been harvested in the garden.

It had not been a heavy enough frost to damage the vegetables that had not yet been harvested.

But it had left a brownish tint against the orange of the pumpkins.

Despite the nip in the air, Eagle Wolf, had left Nicole long enough to take his morning plunge in the river, while she had returned inside the tepee to do her own washing from a basin of water. She had to admit to missing the copper tub in her parents' lovely bathroom back at their home in St. Louis.

Even her aunt Dot and uncle Zeb had a beautiful tub. They also had an outdoor shower they had prepared. One stood in a small cubicle where one could look up and see the sky while tugging on a rope that sent water splashing down from a contraption her uncle had invented.

The water was always cold, but it was fun to take a shower in such a way.

"You are so quiet," Eagle Wolf suddenly said, drawing Nicole's eyes to him. "You are as captivated by my mountain as we Navaho. You feel safe here, do you not? You feel the mountain's embrace?"

"I feel so many things as I ride beside you," Nicole said, smiling at him. "And, yes, I do feel safe and I do feel your mountain's embrace. It is wonderful, Eagle Wolf."

"In this mountain you will find sanctuary as we Navaho have found. When we first came here, we were fleeing the wrath of the white pony soldiers and the United States government, who stole from us all of the land that has been the Navaho's from the beginning of time."

Nicole saw the hardening of his jaw. She knew he was struggling to control his rage over what had been done to his people.

She felt ashamed of her own countrymen, for she had seen how they had wronged the red man, sometimes even worse than those whose skin was black. There was more than one way to enslave a person.

"Let us ride to where I can gather salt for the women of our village," Eagle Wolf said, quickly lifting his head and changing the subject.

"There is salt up on this mountain?" Nicole asked.

"Come with me. I shall show you," Eagle Wolf said, already heading toward a sandstone ridge.

Nicole was always ready and anxious to learn something new.

Tomorrow she would join the women as they worked in the large garden. Last night's light frost was a reminder that there was not much more time to store food for the long winter ahead.

Tomorrow she would help harvest crops for their winter cook pots, while Eagle Wolf would go with his warriors and hunt to provide meat.

He had lifted his nose into the wind today and told her that he could smell snow in the air. When they looked at the higher elevations of the mountain, they saw a fresh dusting of snow.

Nicole thought the snow was beautiful, but she knew that it could bring devastation to the Navaho if they were not prepared with wood at the sides of their lodges, and with food in their storage bins.

She followed Eagle Wolf as he led her down where willows grew in abundance along a gully.

"Moisture is always dripping here, leaving behind a buildup of salt crystals," Eagle Wolf said, pointing to where long spikes of alkaline crystals hung like the icicles Nicole remembered hanging from the roof of her parents' house on the coldest days of winter.

She drew rein as Eagle Wolf brought his horse to a halt. Then she watched while he took a small leather drawstring pouch from his saddlebag and went to where the salt crystals were hanging. With a rock, he easily knocked the salt into his bag.

"Here is all the salt you will need as you learn the art of Navaho cooking," Eagle Wolf said, closing the drawstring pouch and returning it to his saddlebag.

Nicole felt a hot blush rise to her cheeks. "I do not even know how to boil water," she confessed. "My mother never taught me how to cook. Both she and my father were more interested in my getting an education than spending time in the kitchen with my mother."

"You will have a good teacher in Dancing Snow Feather," Eagle Wolf said, going to Nicole and reaching for her reins.

He took them from her and secured them with his own on the low limb of a cottonwood tree, then lifted his arms up for her.

"Come with me," he said thickly. "Let us go and sit beside that shallow stream over there. I will bring a blanket for us to sit upon."

Nicole felt deliciously warm at the mere touch of this man's hands as he helped her from her horse. They had not made love yet and she felt embarrassed that she wanted to so badly. She could almost burst from the need that overwhelmed her when she was with Eagle Wolf.

As he held her in his arms now, their lips so close, Nicole felt dizzy from a hunger she had not known of until she met Eagle Wolf.

"I need you," Eagle Wolf whispered against her lips. "You need me. I can feel it in the way your body quivers and strains against mine. Now is the time, my woman. Now. I want to make love with you."

"And I want to make love with you, too," Nicole said in a strangely husky voice.

They kissed passionately, and Nicole felt overwhelmed by the emotions that swept through her. She knew it was right for her to give herself to this man today.

Soon they would speak vows. Theirs was a love that would endure everything and would last an eternity.

Forgetting the blanket, Eagle Wolf swept Nicole fully into his arms and carried her to the soft moss that spread down the embankment, into the water.

Quickly, they undressed each other, and suddenly Nicole realized that she was nude for the first time in the presence of a man. Her cheeks flushed hot when she looked over and saw Eagle Wolf standing beautifully nude before her, everything about him so masterful.

She gasped when she saw that part of him that would soon be inside her, where no man had been before. He was very well endowed there, and she wondered how it was that he could fit inside her.

But the way she was throbbing, she knew it was meant for them to come together as men and women had done from the beginning of time.

She would not allow herself to be afraid of this first time, for she knew the gentle side of this man. She knew that he would treat her with tenderness as he entered her. She would learn from him the wonders of lovemaking.

He wrapped his arms around her and with his body urged her down onto the moss, which felt so soft and wonderful against her back.

He swept his body over hers, and with a knee gently parted her legs so that he could enter her without having to shove so hard.

He wanted the pain that came with the first time to be brief. He wanted her to remember the good of their first joining, not the bad.

Chapter Thirty

As birds sang overhead in the trees, like soft music being played just for this moment, Nicole lay in her lover's arms, his mouth eager on hers. She had dreamed of being with Eagle Wolf, of making love, and now her dreams were coming true.

As she clung to him, her body yearning for his, she felt the possessive heat of his kiss. Slowly, gently, he thrust his manhood where she was throbbing with a need all new to her.

She held on to him as he gave one last shove, and she felt a slight stabbing of pain upon his entry. But the pain lasted for only a moment. Then, as he began to move gently within her, a pleasure she had never known began to grow within her. She strained her body against his, hungry for more of the exquisite pleasure he was awakening within her.

She instinctively wrapped her legs around his waist, and rode with each of his thrusts. His movements aroused the most wondrous of feelings within her.

"My woman," Eagle Wolf whispered against her lips. "I love you *ka-bike-hozhoni-bi*. Forever-more."

"And I shall love you *ka-bike-hozhoni-bi*," she whispered back to him.

Then he moved more earnestly within her, and she felt the sweetest of currents spreading through her.

She closed her eyes and allowed herself to feel it all as he again kissed her with such passion, she sighed with pleasure. She clung to him, her body moving with his.

She was flooded with emotion as Eagle Wolf swept a hand around one of her breasts and kneaded it so that she felt the nipple grow tight against his palm. She sucked in a breath of utter pleasure when he moved his lips to that same nipple and gently sucked it between his teeth, softly nibbling.

Then he swirled his tongue around it, and again sucked the nipple into his mouth.

"What you are doing is . . . driving . . . me wild," Nicole whispered, feeling heat surge through her whole body, this sensual awakening that was so sweet and wonderful.

"Just enjoy," Eagle Wolf whispered against her cheek. "You feel it all now, do you not? You feel my need for you. You feel my want of you."

"I feel everything wonderful, my darling," Nicole said, gazing up at him through passion-clouded eyes. "My handsome Navaho chief. Oh, how I do love you."

"We were destined to meet and to know a love so fierce it should shake the heavens," Eagle Wolf said, smiling into her eyes. "It should awaken all of nature. Hear the birds? Their songs accompany our love dance."

His lips came down onto Nicole's and kissed her more passionately than before. He swept his arms around her and held her tightly against his body, experiencing something with Nicole that he had never felt before with any other woman, not even his wife.

Now he saw how wrong he had been to marry for the wrong reasons.

This time his wife, his Nicole, would experience everything that love could give. He knew that she would always return his love, twofold, as she was doing today.

She clung and rocked with him, and heat spread through him, a liquid heat that melted his insides. His whole body was quivering with anticipation.

His skin actually tingled with an aliveness he had never felt before. And his stomach was churning wildly.

No, never before had he experienced anything even close to how he was feeling now with this woman.

That day when he lay there so overwhelmed with fever, it was fate that led her to him. Had she not come, his life would never have been complete.

Now that they had found come together, they completed each other.

Nicole was almost mindless with the pleasure that Eagle Wolf was introducing her to. She was feeling a strange sort of pressure building within her.

And then, as his lips came to hers again in a demanding kiss, she arched her back and hugged him tightly to her.

Suddenly it seemed as though lights were flashing inside her brain, and the most delicious feeling swept through her, rocking her with an intensity she had never imagined possible. She clung to him. She sighed. She cried out his name just as he cried out hers against her lips. His body trembled and he thrust himself over and over again inside her, and then lay quietly against her, his breathing as quick as her own.

"What I just felt . . ." she said, marveling over what had happened to her body. It was as if she had been reborn into a new and different world, a world of sensuality.

"I felt the same," Eagle Wolf said, rolling away from her and stretching out on his back on the soft moss. "You just discovered the truth about lovemaking and what can happen inside the body, inside the soul, when you truly love someone as you and I love each other."

He turned on to his side toward her. He bent

his head to her breasts, and swept his tongue around one nipple and then the other, feeling the heat of her flesh against his lips.

Nicole threw her head back and closed her eyes in ecstasy as Eagle Wolf then kissed her lips with a warmth and passion that would always be there.

She would always need him.

She would always love him.

She twined her fingers through his long black hair, loving the feel of it against her hand. Then she swept her hands across his muscled back, stopping at his buttocks, where she splayed her fingers across his flesh.

"Your body is so magnificent," she murmured as he leaned his face away from hers, his eyes gazing intently into hers.

"Your body is more than that," Eagle Wolf said, laughing huskily. "I cannot keep my hands or lips off you."

"I am yours, for always," Nicole murmured, closing her eyes in ecstasy again when he kissed first one breast, and then the other.

They were abruptly startled away from each other when they heard a noise behind them, in the bushes.

All Nicole could think of was Sam Partain!

Had he found his way onto the mountain? Had he observed their lovemaking, only to kill them afterward?

She knew that the knife Eagle Wolf always

carried in a sheath at his hip was now with his clothes and hers, too far away for him to grab it.

His rifle was in the gun boot on his horse.

They were defenseless.

Both sat up quickly.

Nicole trembled as she covered her bare breasts with her hands and looked toward the bushes where the noise had come from.

Eagle Wolf sat beside her, his hand inching out toward his sheathed knife. But he realized that it was too far away for him to get it without leaving Nicole's side. That might give whatever was there time to attack Nicole in his absence.

He could not chance it.

Suddenly they both saw a pair of golden eyes through a break in the bushes. Both recognized those eyes at the same moment.

"The wolf," Nicole gasped out as Eagle Wolf whispered the same.

"It's the wolf I've seen before," Nicole said, wondering why the animal continued to stand there. "I recognize it by that large scar."

"It is the same wolf that I have also seen many times before," Eagle Wolf said, his eyes looking deeply into the wolf's. "It is the very one that I saved those many sleeps ago. It has appeared to me since then more than once."

"Yet . . . yet . . . it is not attacking either of us," Nicole said, her voice trembling with fear.

"We are not what it seeks," Eagle Wolf said, just as the wolf turned and ran away from them.

It was soon lost from sight in the shadows of the aspen forest.

Nicole sighed with relief. She scambled to her feet, went to her clothes and hurried into them while Eagle Wolf did the same.

"You said that you saved the wolf," Nicole murmured. "How?"

"The wolf came to me that day, injured from a fight. It trusted me enough to allow me to use medicine on it, herbs from the forest that my shaman taught me how to find. Since then it has appeared to me many times, but it's never come as close to me again as it did on the day that I found it near death."

"I saw the wolf when I was all alone on the mountain. I was afraid that it would attack me, yet it didn't," Nicole murmured. "It gave me a look that I could not comprehend, and then went on its way. It appeared to me more than that one time. It is so mystical a creature, Eagle Wolf. I just cannot help wondering why it appears, yet never attacks. I see that as a miracle."

"The miracle is that the wolf survived its wounds," Eagle Wolf said, taking Nicole by the hand and leading her to her mare. "Although I did what I could for it, I doubted it would survive. It had lost a lot of blood."

"Yet there it was again today," Nicole said, mounting her steed while Eagle Wolf went and mounted his own. "It's quite a mystery."

"I believe the wolf is on a hunting expedition,"

Eagle Wolf said, riding away from the stream at Nicole's side.

"A hunting expedition?" Nicole repeated. "For food?"

"No, for whatever scarred it in such a horrendous way," Eagle Wolf answered, slowly nodding. "I pity the enemy, two-legged or four-legged, that is the reason for its restlessness. If the wolf did not have this need, it would have returned to others of its own kind."

"I had always thought that wolves were quite fearful of humans," Nicole said, now riding through tall, blowing, sandy-colored grass.

"Wolves normally are afraid of humans, and stay away from them, but from all that I see about this wolf, it is very different," Eagle Wolf said, looking over his shoulder in the direction where he had last seen the wolf. "I do wonder sometimes why it seeks me out as it has more than once."

"Because it sees you as a friend," Nicole murmured. She smiled softly. "I believe I am seen as a friend, too, for the wolf has never threatened me."

"Perhaps it senses your feelings toward me," Eagle Wolf said, now guiding his steed into a forest of aspens.

"But how?" Nicole asked, following behind Eagle Wolf because there was no room to ride beside him.

"That is where mysticism comes into play," Eagle Wolf said, smiling over his shoulder at her. "My woman, as you live among my people you will be exposed to many things that puzzle you, but always remember that there is a reason for everything and there is always something or someone to watch over you."

"I feel it already," Nicole said, returning his smile. "And I feel so blessed because of it . . . because of you."

"I hunt tomorrow while you help in the garden. Soon there will be a wedding for my people to celebrate," Eagle Wolf said. "Ours, my woman. Ours."

That made Nicole feel a sense of happiness and peace that she had never known before, and it was all because of a man most whites would kill if they saw him riding alone in the forest.

That thought made her shudder with a strange, sudden fear that was new to her.

Chapter Thirty-one

The campfire was burning low as Sam Partain and his men got up to begin a new day of their search.

But things had changed. Several of the men who had ridden with him on his quest to find Nicole Tyler had left angrily in the night.

They had tried to talk Sam into forgetting this nonsense and letting the woman be. When he refused to listen to reason, they snuck away in the darkness.

Now there were only two men riding with Sam, their eyes set on the upper slopes of the mountain.

Searching farther and farther up the mountain had become Sam's obsession. He would not let the fear of Navaho Injuns spook him out of getting his revenge.

But he had decided that if he hadn't found Nicole in the next two days, he would finally give up on her and return with his friends to St. Louis. The nights had already proven that winter was not far away. The higher elevations of the mountain were already snow-shrouded.

"Sam, can't you feel how cold it is this morning?" Ace asked as Sam kicked the last of the dirt on the campfire until all the glowing embers were covered. "Take a gander up yonder. Snow, Sam. There's more snow on the peaks than yesterday. Don't that give you a hint of what's to come? Sam, two more days are two days too many for me. I don't trust this mountain. It's haunted by Injuns. Who's to say when a hard snowfall will suddenly come and cover us like thick, white blankets, sent by the spirits of this damn mountain? Navaho spirits, Sam."

"You believe in too much superstitious fluff," Sam said, laughing contemptuously as he placed his blanket in his saddlebag. "Come on. Get in your saddle and let's go. The sun will soon warm you through and through. You'll forget the chill of the night. And as for snow? Good Lord, man, it's too early in the season to think about it, much less cause me to give up my search for the Tyler woman."

Ace gave Tom a harried look, hoping the other man would back him up. Maybe Tom could come up with some argument that would stop Sam from continuing this idiotic search for a woman who meant nothing at all to Tom, or Ace.

Tom just shrugged and mounted his horse, and Ace had no choice but to follow him.

They gave Sam a harried look, then rode farther up the mountain pass that they had found only yesterday. It was worn enough to tell them that it was used frequently, no doubt by the Navaho, who were the only ones who came this far up the mountain.

Sam supposed that knowledge should have sent him running for cover, but he was too intent on finding Nicole to care. Once he did, he would get out of this place as fast as his horse would carry him.

He wasn't as dumb as his friends thought him to be. He knew that he was chancing everything in order to take his revenge.

"She's got to be on this mountain," Sam grumbled as he snapped his horse's reins. "We've been all over lookin' for her. No prints lead farther than this mountain. They're hers, you know it. We followed them from where she was last. In that Mormon community. I might not be an Injun, but damn it, I'm skilled at trackin' horses' prints. And she just can't have gotten far. We'll find her today or my name ain't Sam Partain."

Suddenly Sam went quiet as he spied something that made him stare with disbelief.

The wolf!

It had to be the same wolf that he had left for dead some months ago after it had come up on him while he was alone at a river.

He was stunned that the wolf had lived after what Sam had done to it. Why, Sam had practically skinned it after stabbing the son of a gun in the side.

He'd left the wolf for dead, and then he and his

friends had hightailed it outta there quicklike in case the wolf ran with a pack that might attack them.

The last time he had looked back at that wolf, it was lying in its life blood, but Sam had noticed that it was still breathing, its golden eyes following Sam's every move. Sam had thought to go back and put it out of its misery by shooting it. But instead, he had laughingly gone on his way, leaving the wolf half alive.

Damn it, how on earth had that wolf stayed alive?

He grabbed for the rifle in his gun boot, but the wolf was gone in a flash, like a ghost that might materialize and then disappear just as quickly.

A chill rode his spine. What if that had been the ghost of a wolf, come back to haunt Sam?

"What're you staring at?" Ace asked as he came up beside Sam's horse. "Why, Sam, you're as pale as a spook. What scared you?"

"It's the damnedest thing," Sam said, idly scratching his brow. "You know that wolf I told you about while we were on our way to Tyler City? The one I left to die?"

"Yeah, what about it?" Ace asked, lifting an eyebrow.

"Well, if'n I didn't know better, I'd believe I just saw that same damn wolf peering out at me from those bushes over yonder," he said, pointing with the barrel of his rifle to where he was sure that he had seen the animal. "It has to be the same one. The deep scar, where no fur grows, shows where I cut that damn wolf. I just know it. It is the same critter."

"So it lived—" Ace shrugged. "What of it? When you get the chance, shoot it and this time make certain it's dead. I don't like the idea of being stalked by a damn, angry wolf."

"Me neither," Tom said as he came to Sam's other side. "In fact, gents, let's hunt that rascal down and make sure it's dead this time."

"That's a good idea," Sam growled. He slid his rifle back into his gun boot. The three men took off at a fast clip on their horses in the direction Sam had last seen the wolf running.

But no matter how far they rode, or in which direction, they didn't find the wolf.

"Well, that's that," Sam said, disgruntled. "It's given us the slip. But keep an eye out for it. I can't imagine that thing leaving me alive after what I done to it."

"Another reason we should turn back and hightail it to St. Louis," Ace said, glaring at Sam. "Sam, I'm tired of this. I'm leavin' you now. I've had it. The thought of that wolf out there is enough to spook me into sayin' good-bye until we meet again in St. Louis."

He looked over at Tom. "Joining me?" he asked. "Had enough?"

"Yep, I'd say so," Tom said, swinging his horse around and heading it back down the mountain.

He looked over his shoulder at Sam. "See ya in hell, Sam, for sure enough, if that wolf has anything to do with it, that's where you're gonna wind up. It's just waitin' for the right moment to jump out at ya."

Sam stared disbelievingly at Ace as he joined Tom on the trek downward. "You're both cowards!" he shouted as he waved a fist at them. "I ought to shoot you for deserting me."

"I wouldn't fire that gun if I wuz you," Ace said. "That would sure enough let the Navaho know they were no longer alone on their mountain."

"The mountain don't belong to the Navaho," Sam shouted angrily at him. "It's everyone's."

"Including the wolf's," Ace said, then rode away from Sam with Tom alongside him.

Sam felt bewildered by what had just happened. First he saw what he knew was that same wolf that he had left to die, and then the rest of his friends deserted him?

He heard a rustling behind him.

He turned with a start and gasped. He felt the color drain from his face when he saw the wolf step out from behind the bushes, its golden eyes intent on him.

Sam's fingers trembled as he yanked his rifle from the gun boot again, and took aim. But just as quickly as before, the wolf was gone again, as though it knew the art of disappearing into thin air.

"You gol'darn animal," Sam said, breathing hard.

He glanced over his shoulder in the direction his friends were going. He then looked again where he had seen the wolf.

"No wolf is going to get the best of me," he whispered to himself.

He held on to his rifle as he rode onward. He kept watching for the wolf on all sides, but still he didn't see it.

"Sneaky son of a gun, ain'tcha?" he said, trying to shake off the fear he was feeling.

He looked over his shoulder again. Something told him that he was making a mistake by not joining his friends, but when Sam Partain made up his mind to do something, gol'darn it, he did it.

Suddenly he heard the yip-yipping of several wolves. It seemed there was not only that one to keep an eye out for, but a whole pack.

His teeth chattered from fear. He tried to blame it on the temperature, which today was colder than yesterday.

He stopped long enough to take a jacket from his saddlebag and put it on. As he started forward again, he heard yip-yipping on first one side of him, and then the other.

Chills rode his spine. He seemed to be riding right toward the wolves' cries.

And then once again he caught sight of the very one he had injured. It came from behind the bushes once again, as though to purposely taunt

Sam. Again, it disappeared as soon as Sam lifted his rifle.

"You lousy, sneaky animal!" Sam cried, his eyes darting in all directions. All he could see were golden-leafed aspen trees, and all he could hear was the rush of water coming from a waterfall that must be nearby.

He had never felt so alone, or so vulnerable.

If only he could be at a gambling table, cards in hands, money spread out in front of him, as he taunted the other players he knew would lose to him.

He began trembling when he saw the wolf again, but this time if was not standing still, staring at him. It was running up ahead, again as though taunting him.

When it stopped and gave Sam a look, Sam saw it as one of defiance, and . . . and . . . of victory.

It was then that Sam knew he had finally lost his largest gamble of all . . . life!

He screamed when wolves appeared on all sides of him.

He had already fainted dead away when he was knocked from his horse and his neck was slit open by sharp teeth. The wolves howled in victory over a human being that had no place on this earth any longer.

Chapter Thirty-two

Snow was suddenly falling in white sheets outside Nicole and Eagle Wolf's tepee. She was troubled because Eagle Wolf had left the village before it started snowing. He and several of his warriors had gone to hunt for smaller game, since the main hunt had been such a success only a month ago.

"Dancing Snow Feather, you don't look at all concerned about the sudden snowfall," Nicole murmured as she knelt beside the lovely pregnant woman. She and her sister-in-law were making kneel-down bread for their husbands.

Yes, Nicole was now married to the man she absolutely adored.

She couldn't be happier except for when she looked at Dancing Snow Feather's belly, which was growing round with child. Nicole knew that she wanted to be pregnant, too.

She couldn't understand why she hadn't become with child, too. Ever since speaking their vows, she and Eagle Wolf had made love almost every night, yet she still wasn't pregnant!

She knew how much her husband wanted children. In fact, Nicole had actually become somewhat alarmed after they were married because he kept talking about the children he was anxious to have with her.

She had one evening suddenly recalled how he had said that his marriage to his first wife was one of convenience only, and that he had mainly been concerned about her giving him sons.

Nicole had begun to worry that he had not married her for the right reasons, but just because he needed sons.

She knew how important it was to the Navaho to have children. Some whites called them a "vanishing people" because so many had been slain by the cavalry.

Of course, both girls and boys were needed to build the numbers of the Navaho again, but it was sons that Eagle Wolf always spoke of.

When she had told him her fears on this, that he might have married her for the wrong reasons, he had taken her quickly into his arms and convinced her otherwise. He had spoken softly and sweetly to her and made love in a way that left no doubt as to his feelings for her.

She no longer worried about his reasons for marrying her. She knew now that he loved her for herself. Having children with her would only be something that would make their relationship even more precious.

"Nicole?"

Dancing Snow Feather's sweet voice broke through Nicole's thoughts. "What did you say, Dancing Snow Feather?" Nicole asked, pausing for a moment in her bread making.

"You were so deep in thought," Dancing Snow Feather said, wiping cornmeal from her hands on the doeskin apron she wore to protect her pretty beaded dress.

"I'm sorry," Nicole said, wiping her hands on her own doeskin apron. Dancing Snow Feather had taught her how to make not only that, but also dresses and moccasins.

She had also taught Nicole how to make Eagle Wolf fancy buckskin vests that were embellished with colorful feathers hanging from the hem.

Nicole was an astute student, but she was also a teacher. She taught the Navaho children now five days a week in a log lodge that had been built by the warriors of the village. Everyone was anxious for their children to learn what white children were taught, so that the Navaho would no longer be at a disadvantage when they might have to deal with whites in the future.

Nicole was proud that some of the men and women of the village also came into the classroom and were learning from her, too.

In fact, a larger building was being readied, so that she would have one building for the adults, and one for the children. She was happy to oblige, for she loved teaching anyone who would listen to her lessons.

"I know that you are worried about our husbands being out in this heavy snowfall, but do not be afraid," Dancing Snow Feather murmured. "They know this land well. No storm will keep them away from their families. Soon you will see them return with many rabbits in their bags. In fact, Nicole, this is a good time to hunt for rabbits, for their tracks will lead our warriors to them."

"When the snow gets heavier, what do you do when you are all forced to stay inside your lodges both day and night?" Nicole murmured.

"There are many games played inside the lodges beside the fire," Dancing Snow Feather said, again busy making her bread. She was stirring up a water and corn mixture, after the corn had been ground to the consistency of flour.

Green corn husks had been readied ahead of time and spread open. Now Dancing Snow Feather was pouring some of the mixture into the husks. She then wrapped the husks tightly together, tied them, and set them aside.

"But now that you are here with your teachings, the children will be in school. Half the day will be spent in learning, and then at night they will either share what they learned with their mothers and fathers, or they will play games," Dancing Snow Feather said. "The children and adults are never without something to do until the warm winds of spring arrive again."

Dancing Snow Feather noticed that Nicole had

not resumed making bread, but had gone quiet. She was now staring at Dancing Snow Feather's belly, which was just now big enough to be visible beneath her doeskin dress.

"May I touch it?" Nicole suddenly blurted out.

Dancing Snow Feather smiled. "*Ho*, you may," she said softly. "Give me your hand."

Nicole reached out and Dancing Snow Feather took it and slid it up beneath the apron, so that Nicole's hand was square over the tiny ball where the baby lay.

"My goodness," Nicole gasped. She had never felt a woman's pregnant belly before. She was an only child, so she had never shared moments like this with her mother.

She was awed by the wonder of this new life. Then she felt sad that she did not have the same sort of miracle to share with her husband.

Tears in her eyes, Nicole slid her hand away. "I wonder why I haven't been able to get pregnant," she said, her voice breaking. "Eagle Wolf wants children so badly. And . . . so . . . do I. I love children."

"I can tell that you do by the way you treat the children you teach," Dancing Snow Feather said, resuming the preparation of her kneel-down bread.

She would later go outside, where a pit had been prepared for the bread. Live coals waited there even now, keeping the pit hot.

The live coals would be removed just prior to

placing the filled corn husks in the pit. Then the bread would be allowed to bake slowly.

Once the bread was fully baked, the loaves would be removed from the pit oven. The hot husks would be stripped away, revealing a wonderful loaf of bread that was ready to be eaten.

"My mother did not have an easy time getting pregnant," Dancing Snow Feather murmured. "She was advised by our shaman what the problem might be."

"And the problem was?" Nicole asked.

"At that time, our shaman was called Swift Star. He told my mother that she was worrying too much about not being with child. Swift Star said all that worry stopped the child from coming," Dancing Snow Feather murmured. She stopped and gazed into Nicole's green eyes. "Stop thinking about it and then it will happen."

"Truly?" Nicole asked, her eyes widening.

Then both looked toward the closed entrance flap when they heard the neighing of horses outside Nicole's tepee. With the snow so soft and thick, neither of them had heard the approaching horse.

But now the neighing came loud and clear, and Nicole knew that her husband's white stallion was right outside her lodge.

She wiped her hands on her apron again and stood quickly. Just when she reached the flap, Eagle Wolf was there, off his horse, and opening it himself.

"Eagle Wolf?" Nicole asked. She saw a strange look on his face as he entered. It was the sort of look he got when he was concerned about something.

She glanced quickly over at Dancing Snow Feather. The other woman leaped quickly to her feet and came to stand beside Nicole, her eyes searching Eagle Wolf's.

"No, do not tell me that you have brought bad news about my husband . . . your brother. . . ." Dancing Snow Feather said, her hands suddenly on her belly, as though to protect her child from whatever she might hear.

"No, it is not about my brother, but someone else," Eagle Wolf said. He reached a hand out for Dancing Snow Feather and gently laid it on her shoulder. "I am sorry if I worried you. My brother is right outside my lodge on his horse. He is waiting there with the other warriors, for we will be leaving again."

"You will?" Nicole asked. "Why are you leaving again after just returning home?" Nicole was more puzzled by the minute at her husband's strange behavior. "Did you not get enough rabbits? If not, why did you return home? And why is that strange look in your eyes?"

"We found a man," Eagle Wolf said thickly. "He has been dead for some time, yet his face is still recognizable. Nicole, I would like for you to come with me and identify him."

"What?" Nicole gasped, feeling her face drain of color. "Why would you want me . . . ?"

"I believe it is the man whose name is Sam Partain, the one responsible for killing everyone in Tyler City," Eagle Wolf said.

"Why would you think that?" Nicole asked, searching his eyes.

"You have spoken of this man several times. You have described him to me in case he might come on our mountain," Eagle Wolf said tightly. "This man has the golden color of hair that you described and it is long."

Nicole shuddered at the thought of Sam Partain lying in the snow, frozen and dead.

"He is alone," Eagle Wolf said. "He seems to have been attacked by some animal, perhaps a wolf."

"A wolf?" Nicole repeated, recalling the wolf that she had seen so many times now. "Do you think it was . . . our . . . wolf?" she blurted out. "It always seems so gentle."

"Both you and I have thought that it seemed to be looking for something," Eagle Wolf said thickly. "Or someone. *Ho*, I believe this is the work of that wolf. I believe it finally found vengeance against the one who left it for dead."

"I wonder where she is now," Nicole murmured. She and Eagle Wolf had recently realized that the wolf was a female. They had noticed that its teats seemed larger, of late. It might indicate that she had pups hidden somewhere, and in the snow, that was not good.

"She is smart and she will be all right," Eagle Wolf said softly. "So will her pups if she has given birth to some."

He reached for her hands. "It is not as cold out now as earlier," he said, searching her eyes. "Are you up to going with me to see the face of this man? If he is Sam Partain, you will never have to worry about him again."

"But he was alone?" Nicole murmured. "Are you certain of that?"

"There is only one body out there. If others were with him, I believe seeing him attacked by a wolf gave them cause to retreat as quickly as they could from the mountain. They will not return again," Eagle Wolf said.

Nicole removed her apron. She went to where her warmest coat lay with the blankets that were rolled up along the back of the tepee. She snuggled into the coat, which had been sewn with fur on the inside to keep her warmer.

Then she went and gave Dancing Snow Feather a soft hug. "Can you finish the bread by yourself now that I must leave?" she asked softly.

"Go," Dancing Snow Feather murmured. "Go and see the face. If it is the man Eagle Wolf thinks it is, you will be able to rest better at night from now on."

She drew Nicole closer and whispered into her

ear, "Perhaps now you can concentrate on a baby?"

Nicole returned the hug, then stepped away from Dancing Snow Feather with a smile and a nod. Outside, the sun had just come out from behind the clouds, the snowstorm having moved on down the mountain.

"Let's go," she said, just as a young brave brought her mare to her.

She rode off among the warriors, with Eagle Wolf close beside her.

When they reached the spot where several warriors guarded the dead man, Nicole did not hesitate to dismount and go to take a look at his face.

"Yes, it is Sam Partain," she said, feeling a new sense of peace soar through her. She knew that now she would now be able to focus on what was important to her, for the man she hated and dreaded with every fiber of her being was dead and could hurt no one else again.

"And now who loses at this last game of chance, a gamble that you undertook so recklessly?" Nicole said, kicking snow onto his frozen face.

From somewhere in the distance, Nicole heard the sound of yip-yipping, which she now knew was the way wolves communicated with one another. She smiled, for she knew that this time, the wolves were singing a happy song, a song of victory.

Chapter Thirty-three

It felt so good to Nicole to be back in the warmth of the tepee after having been out in the cold.

Now that she knew Sam Partain was dead, she felt as though she had been set free from the nightmare that he'd created when he killed her parents so coldheartedly, as well as everyone else who lived in Tyler City.

Now Nicole was all calm and peace inside her heart. She could think of nothing except making love with her husband.

She remembered what Dancing Snow Feather had told her . . . that if Nicole could find a way to totally relax and think of nothing but how much she loved Eagle Wolf, she would more than likely get pregnant with that child she and her husband wanted so badly.

With a mischievous glint in her eyes, Nicole stood before the fire and began removing her dress as Eagle Wolf watched, his eyes filled with wonder.

"It is only midafternoon, my wife, and you want to make love?" he asked, enjoying this new side of her as she tossed her dress aside on the floor mats.

"*Ho*, my husband, I want to make love," Nicole murmured, leaning over to remove one moccasin and then the other.

When she was totally nude, she stepped closer to Eagle Wolf and slid her hands up inside his fringed buckskin shirt. She ran her fingers slowly over his sleek, muscled chest. She knew that he was enjoying it when she felt the tingling of his skin everywhere she touched.

Eagle Wolf reached for her hand and slid it out from beneath his shirt. Then he led her down on the thick pallet of furs and blankets beside the lodge fire, where they had made love earlier this morning.

But now there seemed more intensity, more eagerness, on Nicole's part. He saw a new look in her eyes. She smiled confidently at him as he ran his eager hands over her body, stopping to lift one of her breasts closer to his lips so he could flick his tongue around the nipple.

"Husband, please, please undress yourself," Nicole said, her heart hammering. "Or do you want me to do it for you?"

Smiling down at her, Eagle Wolf hurriedly removed his clothes. Without hesitation, he stretched his body over hers and slid his throbbing manhood into her sheath. She was wet and ready for him.

"Love me," Nicole whispered sweetly as she

twined her arms around his neck, bringing his lips down to hers.

She flicked her tongue across his lips, then joined their mouths. His arms swept around her and held her close as they savored the feel and taste of each other's tongues and lips.

"You are so eager," Eagle Wolf whispered against her lips without missing one stroke inside her. He felt the warmth spread almost to a feverish heat throughout his body.

She arched her back so that he could delve more deeply inside her, to touch that part of her that always made her go almost mindless.

"Today I know that we are making a child," Nicole said, leaning away enough so their eyes could meet and hold. "That is what is fueling my eagerness. Eagle Wolf, I can almost feel the child inside me now. I know that what we are doing will bring our longed-for child into the world."

"I will not ask why you believe this," Eagle Wolf said, driven by the heat of passion. "It is just good that you believe it is so."

"I know it is," Nicole murmured, a tremor quaking through her when he brought his lips to hers again and gave her an all-consuming kiss.

As he continued thrusting inside her, she sucked in breaths of rapture, her eyes closed now. She was filled with sensations she had never felt before; she felt as though she herself had just been reborn.

She had never felt so alive, so filled with absolute joy, and it was because she was letting herself go as she had never done before.

She clung to him.

She rocked with him.

She returned his kisses as his arms enfolded her and carried her with him into this new world of complete oneness.

"I love you so," Eagle Wolf whispered against her lips. The press of his mouth was so warm, so deliciously inviting.

"I shall love you forever and ever," Nicole whispered back, then moaned when she felt herself reaching a level of passion that she had never felt before.

She clung even more fiercely to him when he moved his lips down to one of her breasts, his mouth closing over it. Then he swirled his tongue around the nipple, his teeth nipping.

Eagle Wolf felt the fire spreading within him, as never before. It was so intense a feeling, it dazzled his senses.

He slid his lips up to the curve of her neck and pressed them there, panting as the heat of his manhood continued to thrust within her. She rode with him, her legs wrapped around his waist, molding her closer to the contours of his muscled, copper body.

They moved together rhymically now, both breathing hard, and then the peak of their passion was reached. Their bodies experienced delicious shivers of desire, leaving them clinging and breathless, even shaking, it was so intense an experience. Never before had they known such fulfilment.

"I believe you," Eagle Wolf said huskily as he rolled away from Nicole. He rested on his back, gazing through the smoke hole over head, where the sky was blue and peering back at him, a witness, it seemed, to these lovers who had found the ultimate of ecstasy together.

"What do you mean . . . you believe me?" Nicole asked, turning on her side to face him. She slid a hand onto his flat belly and ran her fingers across his wondrous copper skin, causing his flesh to shiver from a pleasure that would not leave him today.

"I believe you now about making a child today," Eagle Wolf said, reaching for and taking her hand. He slid it down to where he still ached for her touch.

When she knew what he wanted, she circled her fingers around his heat and enjoyed the way his manhood grew even larger within her hand when she caressed him like this.

"So, you, too, feel it," Nicole murmured. "How our lovemaking was freer this time than other times, how I seemed not to have a worry in the world? How I adored every moment we made love? My darling Eagle Wolf, it was different this time because I no longer have the worries that have stood in the way of my becoming with child. Now that the evil man who murdered my parents is gone, I no longer have to think of him and where he might be. I was always so afraid that he might still be after me."

"You were right. I am amazed that he found his way onto our mountain despite all of my trained sentries," Eagle Wolf said, reaching down and moving her hand gently aside. It was not needed any longer. He was ready to go to paradise with his wife again, and if a child was not made that first time, it would be the second.

"I believe the wolf that you saved that day is responsible for the death of Sam Partain," Nicole said, groaning with a building pleasure when Eagle Wolf slid over her and quickly thrust his heat inside her again. "I believe it was Sam Partain who inflicted those injuries on that wolf. I believe that all along the wolf was searching for Sam Partain."

"Shhh," Eagle Wolf said as he softly slid a hand over her mouth. "There is no need to think of that man again, or why or how he died. It is enough that he is dead."

"*Ho*, it is enough," Nicole said, her heart thumping inside her chest as the rapture rose inside her with each of Eagle Wolf's thrusts.

She knew that this time paradise would be reached much more quickly than moments ago, for her body was still throbbing from its intense pleasure.

She twined her arms around his neck and felt a tremor deep within herself as Eagle Wolf's lips came to hers, his lips hot and hungry as he kissed her.

Yet her mind would not focus only on love-making this time as it had the first time they had reached paradise together this afternoon.

Suddenly she was filled with curiosity about the wolf.

"I wonder where she is," she suddenly said, causing Eagle Wolf's eyes to widen and his body to grow still for the moment.

"Where who is?" he asked incredulously.

"The wolf," Nicole said, searching his eyes.

"You are not supposed to be thinking about wolves, or anything else, right now," Eagle Wolf said.

"When we are through, can we go out and search for her?" Nicole asked, her eyes wide as he gazed into them. "I do care."

"As do I," Eagle Wolf said thickly. "*Ho*, my wife, mother of the children we are certain to have, we shall go and search."

He reached for her hair and ran his fingers slowly through the radiant red softness of it. "Will that make you happy?" he asked.

"*Ho*, that will make me happy," Nicole said, smiling almost timidly at his patience even when she interrupted their moments of passion with worries about an animal.

But strangely enough, her worry, about not being with child was no longer there. Like magic, the concern had disappeared. She had no doubt that in nine months, a child would be born of their love.

She hoped that in nine more months, another child would be born. She did not want an only child as she had been. It just was not fair to raise a child without a brother or sister.

If her first child were a girl, she would want a brother for her. She had heard that brothers were such a blessing to a sister, protecting her until she found a man to marry. Even then, the bond between brother and sister was never broken.

Not until death. And even then the bond continued in spirit as Eagle Wolf had explained about his sister.

Again they rocked together, clinging, kissing, and reeling with the building pleasure. Nicole was keenly aware when that familiar delicious languor began to swim through her. Soon she would feel the completeness of passion once again with her husband.

And when it did come, his eyes went dark with emotion as he gazed into hers while thrusting over and over again inside her. The silent explosion of their passion made them cling until their bodies grew still once again against each other.

"My hero," Nicole said as he rolled away from her, remaining on his side so that he could gaze at her.

"Your hero?" Eagle Wolf asked, arching an eyebrow.

"*Ho*, my hero," Nicole said, smiling sweetly at

him. "You are my knight in shining armor who came and rescued me when I needed rescuing the most."

When she saw that he did not understand the word "knight," she smiled into his eyes and explained the meaning to him.

And then he said something that surprised her.

"Have you never thought about how strange it is that you were given a name by your parents that had no true meaning?" he asked, placing a gentle hand on her cheek.

"No, I never thought about that," Nicole replied. "My parents named me after a distant aunt." She laughed softly. "And, no, there is no particular meaning behind that name. Why do you ask?"

"Because, my woman, my wife, my people never give names without meanings behind them," he said softly. "Eagle? Wolf? On the day of my birth, as I was told, my mother saw an eagle soaring overhead outside the tepee, and my father heard the baying of a wolf. Those two creatures were honored when they named me."

"I don't know anything about what happened on the day of my birth, so there could be no true meaning behind my name," Nicole said, sighing.

"I will give you a name," Eagle Wolf said, sitting up. He took her hands and urged her to sit before him, their eyes locked.

"But how will you know what to name me?" Nicole asked, searching his eyes.

"I will give you a name that I believe defines

you," Eagle Wolf said. "Whispering Doe. You are as gentle and beautiful as a doe, and from our first meeting your heart has whispered to mine. I would like to call you Whispering Doe."

"Why, that is so beautiful," Nicole murmured. "I love it."

"Then from now on you will be called Whispering Doe," he said. Then his eyes shifted quickly to the closed entrance flap. "Did you hear that?"

Nicole had heard a soft yip-yipping outside their tepee.

"Could it be . . . ?" she asked, hurrying into her dress and moccasins as Eagle Wolf pulled on his fringed breeches and moccasins.

They went outside together, both gasping when they found the female wolf lying on her side behind their tepee. A tiny, lone offspring was suckling on her teat.

It was an incredible sight. They were amazed that the wolf had brought its one baby so close to humans, but soon they saw why. The long wound on the mother's side had somehow become opened and was oozing blood.

"She brought her baby to us because she thought she might not live long enough to keep it alive herself," Nicole said, a sob catching in her throat. She looked quickly over at Eagle Wolf. "I wonder if she got wounded again by Sam Partain."

"I would imagine so," Eagle Wolf said.

"We must do something, but what?" Nicole

asked. "I doubt she will allow us to take her and her baby into the tepee. She only knows the life of the wild."

"She sees us as friends, or she would have not came to us for help. I believe she will welcome the warmth of our lodge, and food," Eagle Wolf said, stepping closer to the wolf, to test her reaction.

When the wolf did not shy away from him, or take her baby in her mouth to carry it away, Eagle Wolf sensed that she was giving permission for him to do as he saw fit.

"Whispering Doe, you carry the pup and I will carry the mother," Eagle Wolf said thickly.

Nicole did not hesitate to reach for the tiny, sweet thing. Meanwhile, Eagle Wolf lifted the mother wolf into his arms and hurriedly took her to the warmth of the lodge.

"I healed her wound before. I shall do it again," Eagle Wolf said, as he laid the wolf on a blanket beside the fire. "Hold the tiny thing while I administer to the mother's wound. Then we can put them together again, but this time they will be where it is warm, and where they both will be cared for."

Nicole gazed with intense love at Eagle Wolf. She had never known anyone as kind and compassionate as her husband.

She sat down with the tiny animal in her arms and watched Eagle Wolf with the mother wolf, amazed at how the animal put such trust and faith in Eagle Wolf. Creatures of the wild were not prone to trust human beings.

But Eagle Wolf was not just any human being. He was special, in all ways different from any white man she had ever known. She wished that her father had been born with the same understanding of what the world was all about. If he had been, he would never have wasted his time at the gambling table. And he would surely be alive today.

Chapter Thirty-four

Several years later

Spring was sweet in the air. The snow on the peaks of the mountain was melting, filling the rivers and streams with freshened water.

Nicole sat outside her tepee beside Dancing Snow Feather, contentedly sewing new vests for their husbands as they watched their children playing.

Nicole could now proudly boast of three children, while Dancing Snow Feather had two of her own.

Altogether there were three daughters and two sons between them, the sons Nicole and Eagle Wolf's. Her belly was big again, for she had been blessed with another child, who should be born in a matter of weeks.

It mattered no longer to Nicole whether or not she had a daughter or son. She had discovered that it was blessing enough to have a healthy child.

"Life is wonderful," Nicole murmured, drawing Dancing Snow Feather's eyes to her. "I could not want for more than what I have been given. I just wish my parents could see and enjoy their grandchildren. Mother couldn't have more than one child."

"I feel blessed, too," Dancing Snow Feather murmured, giggling when the two new pups of the mother wolf came romping around the grown pups, teasing the older ones into nipping at them.

"*Ka-bike-hozhoni-bi*, happy evermore," Nicole murmured.

When she heard horses approaching the village, she watched proudly as Eagle Wolf rode into view. A travois being dragged behind his steed was filled with pelts and meat for his family, while the other warriors followed, with their own trophies from the hunt.

Spirit Wolf rode beside Eagle Wolf, devoted to his brother as no other brother could be.

That made Nicole proud, for she recalled how it had been when she'd first met Spirit Wolf, and how jealousy had turned him bitter and vindictive.

The village remained hidden from the white soldiers. The Owl Clan was still safe.

There were new herds of horses on the mountain. And the large, communal garden had been planted and would provide food for all who lived there.

When Eagle Wolf smiled at Nicole from his white stallion, she melted inside as though it was the first time he had given her such a look.

She whispered the words "I love you" to him so that he could see.

He whispered the words back to her, then rode on with his warriors, so they could unload their prime catches, and divide them among the women.

Nicole could not be any more content than she was. Only occasionally did she allow herself to think about Sam Partain and what he had done to her parents. Although she could not help remembering from time to time, she never allowed such thoughts to ruin the happy life she had now with her husband and children.

She knew that her parents would bless this union between their daughter and the powerful Navaho chief who loved her. And they would absolutely adore their grandchildren!

"See? That's him, that's Black Horse," Gentle Water whispered. She put her hand over her mouth and stifled a giggle.

"Quiet! He might hear us," Meadow warned with a stern glance. She tried to look serious, but the sight of the young war chief on the other side of the thick brush sent her heartbeat racing and caused a strange fluttering sensation in the pit of her stomach. She turned away from Gentle Water and focused on the man down by the riverbank.

Even from this distance he appeared to be slightly taller than most of the Sioux men in their village. Two thin braids wound with brass wires framed his handsome face and dangled over his bare chest. The rest of his dark hair hung to his waist. A large necklace of grizzly-bear claws encircled his neck—potent medicine for a warrior to possess. Black Horse was a chief warrior, which at his young age meant that he held a powerful position in the tribe.

Everything about him was impressive, Meadow noticed. His shoulders were outlined with bulging, sinewy muscles, his belly lean and defined. A white breechcloth encircled his hips, and tan leather leggings hugged his muscular thighs.

"Do you want to meet him now?" Gentle Water asked. Her voice rose slightly above a whisper. She muffled another giggle when her friend shook her fist at her. Gentle

Water leaned close to the other girl. "Your face is red, Meadow. I think you want to do more than just meet him."

"I'm leaving," Meadow whispered through gritted teeth. Before she could turn around to crawl back through the thick brush, a deep voice bellowed from the riverbank below.

"Who's there?"

Meadow instinctively fell down flat on her stomach and held her breath. Pressed against the hard ground, she could feel her heartbeat thudding uncontrollably. Beside her, Gentle Water was also lying facedown in the underbrush. But now she was also being quiet as death. Meadow silently cursed herself for letting Gentle Water talk her into coming down to the river today. Nothing could be more humiliating than getting caught in this compromising position.

When his cry was met with silence, Black Horse grew wary. He pulled his antler-handled knife from the sheath at his hip, bent his knees and began to inch up the sloping riverbank. His dark eyes darted back and forth. The dense brush of alders and willows made it difficult for him to see. Black Horse knew how easy it was to hide in heavy brush such as this. He had done so on many occasions when he had been hunting game, or waiting in ambush for an enemy.

Sensing there was someone—or something—hiding in the bushes, Black Horse didn't call out again. He continued to take cautious steps toward the bushes. He had moved only a few feet, though, when his keen ears picked up the slight sound of rustling brush. His footsteps halted. Every muscle in his body tensed. A light sheen of perspiration broke out on his chest and face as he prepared to go to battle again.

For several moments Black Horse did not move. When another faint sound came from the bushes, he pinpointed his prey's location. He moved like a crouched mountain lion toward the bushes to his left and then peered into the heavy underbrush. He smiled.

Through the low-hanging branches of the willows he could see the distinct forms of two females lying face-down on the ground. He studied them for a moment. Black Horse was certain they were just a couple of curious young girls. His smile widened.

"I must have been imagining things," he said out loud. The girls did not move a muscle. The urge to chuckle tickled the back of his throat, but he resisted.

As he sheathed his knife, he turned and walked back to the river with a nonchalant stride. Humming to himself, Black Horse untied the belt that held his elaborately decorated knife sheath. He placed the weapon down on the ground, then presented his observers with a full view of his hind side as he bent over to pull off his tall, beaded moccasins. He kept his movements slow and provocative. I'll give them something to see, he thought.

Unable to keep the smirk from his lips, Black Horse kept his back to the bushes until he could control his expression. He wanted to make sure that the girls were still watching. He didn't want to waste all this effort if he no longer had an audience. With a feigned look of indifference, he turned around. There were still no signs of movement on the hillside.

Black Horse untied the belt that held up his leggings. He rolled the fringed leg coverings down past his knees, lifted one foot up, then the other, until he was free of the leggings. Clothed only in his breechcloth, he turned toward the river again. He remained in this position for a moment to give the two visitors a chance to leave before they saw more than they were expecting. Or maybe that's what they want, he told himself. Why else would they be hiding in the bushes while he was preparing to take a bath? He turned sideways to the bushes where his audience hid, and slowly untied the strings at his hip.

In the scanty cover of the bushes, Meadow watched every one of Black Horse's movements in breathless awe. He was the most magnificent man she had ever seen, and the way he was undressing was like nothing she had ever witnessed. In the pit of her stomach, and even lower, she felt an unfamiliar ache. Her insides were on fire, and every time Black Horse discarded another article of clothing, the heat within her grew more consuming.

He was facing the bushes now, and Meadow knew there was no way they could leave without being seen. They would have to wait until he was in the water. Then, they could flee. Once they were away from the river, she planned to tell Gentle Water what a troublemaker she was to have suggested this scheme. But now that they were here she could not tear her gaze from the warrior's seductive movements.

His stark white breechcloth made the young chief's smooth skin shine like glistening copper. His legs were long, with well-defined muscles along his thighs and on the backs of his calves. As he moved, every muscle of his body strained and contracted with exact precision. At that moment, Meadow could not have taken her eyes off him even if the bushes around her had caught on fire and burned to the ground.

When the ties that held his breechcloth together were dangling long and loose in his hands, Black Horse was still facing the bushes. He parted his powerful thighs as he slowly pulled the breechcloth out from between his legs and then casually let it drop on the ground at his feet.

Meadow felt perspiration running down her body as she continued to stare. She had seen very young boys running around naked in the village, and she'd helped her adoptive mother prepare dead men for burial. She knew what a male looked like without his breechcloth. But little boys and dead men did not even begin to compare to the virile male who stood at the river's edge now.

Yearnings that Meadow had never experienced before ballooned inside her until she thought she would burst apart. It seemed as if Black Horse knew he had an audience. But that was ridiculous; he had no idea they were hiding here in the bushes. As soon as he dove into the water, they would get away from here, and this embarrassing situation could be forgotten. Even as that thought passed through her mind, Meadow knew there was no way that she would ever be able to forget the sight of this handsome man, who now stood before her naked as a newborn babe.

The gasps coming from the thick brush almost made Black Horse laugh out loud. More than anything, he wished he could see the faces of his inquisitive observers. He knew, however, it would not be long before he would encounter at least one of them again. When he saw them hiding in the underbrush, he had noticed one of them had hair that was the shade of the prairie sun—a half-breed, most likely. She would be easy to find in the Sioux village, where most of the woman had hair as black as midnight.

Smug and filled with satisfaction that he'd given the curious virgins an eyeful, Black Horse lingered for a second longer. As though he had grown bored with the charade, he turned and sauntered to the river's edge. Without pausing, he walked into the cool water until it was up to his hips and then dove under the surface.

Staying completely submerged, he swam out to the middle before coming up for air. He turned back toward the bushes.

A deep laugh escaped Black Horse when he glimpsed the two spies hurrying up the hillside on the other side of the thick clump of bushes. They were both dressed in the long fringed dresses and knee-high moccasins worn by all the females of the tribe, but the thing that caught his attention the most was the alluring way the buckskin dress caressed the curvy hips of the taller one—the one with the long yellow hair.

Black Horse began to splash around in the deep water of the river. He let the cool water wash away the dirt from the last of the long, hard trails he had ridden for the past few months. For a while, he let his mind clear. At dawn this morning he had crossed the Canadian border. He hoped Canada would offer a peaceful haven where he could rest.

Barely more than three months ago he had ridden with his comrades in the battle at Greasy Grass River—the battleground the white men called Little Bighorn. But victory over the long-haired General Custer and his men had been short-lived. Within weeks of that successful attack, Black Horse's people had been defeated again and again.

But for the first time in a long time he had something besides fighting and killing on his mind. He was thinking of the two girls in the bushes, and of the fun he would have when he had a chance to meet the light haired one face-to-face. His mind recalled the way the wavy locks of her flaxen hair had swung back and forth above her shapely hips as she scurried up the hillside. He hoped she looked as enticing from the front as she did from behind. Another carefree laugh escaped from his mouth. He was looking forward to his stay here in Canada.